DESCRIPTION

Ghostly loggers. Eerie mysteries. Who says your forties aren't fabulous?

Cate yearns to rediscover the driven person she used to be. Completely surprised by the oh-so delightful anniversary gift of a divorce, the floundering forty-two-year-old impulsively moves to the mountains above Palm Springs. But after arriving at the nineteenth-century cabin she inherited from her great-aunt, the suddenly single woman is astounded to find it haunted by the spirit of a sexy lumberjack.

Swallowing her skepticism to go all-in on accepting the supernatural, Cate attends the taping of a ghost-hunter show. But with the co-host dying in a freak accident and whispers that it might be murder, she'll need her swoon-worthy specter's otherworldly assistance to solve the suspiciously spooky mystery.

Can Cate and her ethereal sidekick catch a killer or is she digging her own grave?

Life in the Ghost Lane

A Spirited Midlife

Book One

Morgana Dae

Copyright ©2022 Morgana Dae

First Edition

Edited by Barham Editorial

Beta Reader and Proofing: Pippa Wood

Cover design by Natasha Snow

Published by Knight Ever After Publishing LLC

 Created with Vellum

PROLOGUE

"Aunt Sylvia? Should I keep all these photos in here? Or should we try putting them in albums?"

Sitting on a rocking chair with an old wooden box of photographs from my hundred-year-old great-aunt's life in my lap, I trailed my fingertips across the dusty pile. When was the last time I'd held an actual photo in my hand?

My aunt jabbed a gnarled finger at me from where she was lounging with a quilt wrapped around her in an overstuffed chair by the fireplace.

"Be careful with those, Cate. Some are older than me." She let out a sound somewhere between a cough, snort and sputter. "In other words, ancient."

"Oh, stop." I swallowed hard. I hated being reminded that she probably didn't have much time left. "You're doing great."

She grunted then her eyelids drifted closed.

My dumb commentaries never seemed to fail to show up at the worst times. How did I know how she felt? She could barely get around anymore. At least her tiny mountain cabin meant she didn't have to shuffle too far to get from one spot to the next. The

1

loft was off-limits these days, but other than that, most of the home was an open-plan shoebox, the walls made up entirely of knotty-pine with a river rock fireplace taking center stage.

Cozy. Homey. A lovely mountain cabin on a half-acre surrounded by cedars and pines. I probably loved it as much as she did.

The living room was preceded by a small area that was how guests were greeted at the front door, and an equally small area that made up the kitchen. Two bedrooms and a postage-stamped size bathroom completed the layout. The entire cabin couldn't be more than six or seven hundred feet.

I scraped my teeth along my lower lip as I considered my aunt. I hated to bother her while she was resting, but I did need to get going soon. The time I spent with her was precious, since I lived in Los Angeles which was about a two-and-a-half-hour drive away. Unless I drove during rush hour. Then it could be somewhere between three hours and the end of civilization as we know it.

I *never* drove during rush hour.

Plus, I wanted to make sure she was okay before I left. I had to verify that the battery was working properly in her life alert bracelet, make her a sandwich in case she got hungry later, harass her over when the home care worker would be in next and annoy her to the point that she wanted to beat me with her cane.

I hated to admit it, but more than once in the past couple of years, I wished I could stay at the cabin with her instead of going home. Once my daughter, Hailey, had headed off to college, I no longer felt attached to my own house for some reason.

I brushed the disquieting thought aside and returned my attention to the pile of photos, sifting through them carefully. Part of the reason I'd pulled the old box out of the cabinet was so I could help her start organizing her things. She'd been complaining for a while that she couldn't find anything. When I discovered the photos in the wooden box, I thought it might be nice to go through them—maybe identify the mystery people in the pictures so we'd have a family record. Thoughts sprang into my head of putting together scrapbooks and decorating them with cute stickers and dried flowers or...

Yeah. That's never happening.

But I could at least get them sorted and out of the dusty, ancient container that was more likely to give her splinters than be of any real use anymore.

I glanced in the direction of my aunt. Her slack jaw and booming snores signaled how deeply asleep she was. The woman had a good set of lungs on her, that was for sure. No, I shouldn't bother her. And anyway, it was already past three in the afternoon. I determined that even though the hubby would whine about me getting back after his precious dinner hour and he'd have to—*gasp*—figure out what to eat all by his widdle self, no way was I getting stuck in the slow crawl through the desert back to L.A.

Decision made. I would spend a couple more hours going through the pictures, maybe pencil in some names and dates once Aunt Sylvia woke up again. I fired off a text to Vince, sharing my plans. I also added some dinner suggestions that food preparation amateurs could handle, then shut off my phone. The whining could wait for when I got home. Give me something to look forward to.

With that handled, I went back to the photographs. I'm not gonna lie. I love history, love antique stores and historical romance novels. You guessed it—total nerd. So instead of the photo-sorting being a task, it was like an adventure.

The top of the pile contained some pictures of people I actually remembered. I would only need my aunt's help with the dates or events they were from. I sniffed on occasion, holding back the tears that threatened when I spotted a photo of my great-grandma with Aunt Sylvia in her younger years, the two sisters arm in arm as they traveled all over the world. They were *true* adventurers, two peas in a pod.

However, the adventure ended once my great-grandmother married. Aunt Sylvia never went that route, remaining steadfastly single her entire life, and in some ways, I envied her. I wouldn't trade my daughter for anything in the universe, but what if I'd waited longer? What if I'd created my own amazing memories from all *my* worldly travels?

I sighed as I straightened the different piles on the burl-wood table—one for people I knew, the other for complete strangers I might be related to—then reached in to grab the next stack. For whatever reason, this small group of photos was tied together with a faded ribbon and seemed to be much older than the rest.

My hands shook as my throat tightened. Even as the sensations overtook me, I wondered why I was responding so dramatically to this particular bundle of pics. Sure, I'd had a lot on my mind lately, had been feeling overly-sentimental and emotional—something the other half had been more than happy to remind me of constantly—but freaking out over some pictures from Aunt Sylvia's collection bordered on bizarre.

Determined to quit behaving like a drama queen, I tugged on the frayed ribbon, the satiny fabric coming untied to reveal the mystery pictures. I drew my eyebrows together, surprised by the image of a ruggedly handsome, fully bearded man dressed in old-fashioned clothing. He posed emotionless with a large axe in front of an enormous fallen tree. The sepia-tone photo featured an embossed photographer's mark at the bottom, indicating that it had been taken by Smith Bros. Photography in Stagecoach, CA.

Hmm. I wasn't that familiar with the historic town at the base of the San Salvador Mountains, but now I was intrigued. There were several such towns with a rich past dating back to the old west in the area, and it might be fun to poke around some old local museums and learn more.

I don't know why the photograph captured me so. I couldn't make out much detail of the man's face, and of course, the picture wasn't in color, so the most I could tell about his appearance was that he had dark hair, dark eyes and I could picture him on the cover of a historical romance.

I squinted to get a better look at the image. Yes, those were true axe-wielding muscles.

I turned the picture over to check for more clues. In barely legible writing, the cursive shaky and ink faded, it read: 'For my dear mother from your loving son. Joshua, 1879.'

"Okay, Joshua 1879. Whose side of the family are you from?"

A loud creak sounded from the darkened bedroom, and I yelped, dropping the pictures. They fluttered to the ground, and I silently admonished myself for being so easily startled.

"Dammit," I mumbled as I quickly gathered up the old photos. I didn't want to damage them through my carelessness.

"What the heck are you doing, Cate? Those photos shouldn't be handled."

I collected them back on my lap, my cheeks heating as though I'd been caught with my hand in the cookie jar. Forty-one years old or not, with just the right turn of phrase or sharpening of tone, she could jettison me right back to my eight-year-old self.

"I'm sorry, Aunt Sylvia. I was sorting them when I was surprised by a loud creak from the bedroom." I chuckled. "I suppose it's the wood expanding or whatever." As if I knew anything about such things. "Or...contracting?"

Aunt Sylvia snorted. "Either that, or it's the creaking of my joints." She side-eyed the pictures. "Be sure to tie those back up so they don't get mixed in with the others."

My gaze snapped down to the pics. The one on top was this very cabin, only it had to have been from when it was being built. The goat shed in the back wasn't there and there were a couple of large tents in the background.

Aunt Sylvia had bought the place shortly after her sister married. Apparently, she'd vacationed in Squirrel Cove a few times and loved the peaceful calm of the area. I wondered if the pictures were left behind and she'd run across them at some point after she bought the place.

"I'm guessing these are from the original owners?" I shuffled through the pics until I got back to the one with Joshua the lumberjack. "Did this Joshua guy build the cabin? Was it his?"

Aunt Sylvia pursed her lips. "I forgot I left those in there. I shouldn't have put..." She glanced away and I could tell something was bothering her. It was as if she was upset I'd seen them—which seemed ridiculous.

Yet, also intriguing.

"Shouldn't have put what?"

My inner curious cat was at play, but so was my concern that I not inadvertently lose any family history. I'd helped my mom go through my grandmother's things and she'd been so upset when she couldn't identify photos or remember other details of her mother's past, such as whether something was a wedding gift from a beloved friend or what year it was her parents took that special anniversary cruise. I didn't want to repeat the same mistake.

It occurred to me how alike my mother and I were in that way. We wanted to know *all* the things.

Aunt Sylvia stared into the fire, seemingly lost in thought as I waited for her to respond to my query. I lowered my eyes to the photos, moving them around as subtly as I could. I was dying to see what else was there.

"Oh, for heaven sakes, Cate." Aunt Sylvia held out her hand. "Hand them over."

My eyes went wide. "You're not going to burn them, are you?"

"Why the heck would I—"

Crash!

I almost choked on my tongue at the sound of something large falling in the bedroom. I swallowed hard. The very room the loud creak had come from. I let out a shaky laugh. I'd been coming to this cabin for almost forty years. Why was I picking now to suddenly decide it was spooky?

However, when I regarded my aunt to share the laugh, she didn't seem all that jolly. Instead, she appeared rather concerned.

"Aunt Sylvia? What is it?"

She stared at me as if I had antennas growing out of my head. "You heard that?"

"Uh, yeah. Of course." I shrugged. "That's the room the creak came from, too."

She narrowed her eyes. "Huh. I see."

I was glad *someone* did. "Why don't I go check whether anything's broken."

I'll confess I was being the dutiful niece and that was it. Despite already scolding myself for being a scaredy-cat, the last place I wanted to go into right then was that dark, unusually loud room.

I rose, handing her the photos once I was on my feet. I made my way the short distance to her bedroom, then reached in and flipped the light switch before setting one foot across the threshold. I blinked as my eyes adjusted to the brighter surroundings. As I glanced around, I couldn't place what might have caused the loud bang, until I tripped over it. I grabbed one of the posts of her four-poster bed to keep from tumbling to the ground.

I arched my eyebrows at Aunt Sylvia's jewelry box, the culprit that had not only frightened us, but had almost made me break my ankle. Somehow, it had managed to leap off her dresser and land five feet away at the foot of her bed.

There's a completely logical explanation for that.

What it was, I had no clue. It might only be late afternoon, but it felt as if it were midnight, and I was trapped in Count Dracula's castle.

I gingerly righted Aunt Sylvia's jewelry box, worried that the beautiful old item had been broken in the fall. The lid was slightly ajar, but the contents hadn't flown everywhere. As I gathered it in my arms, a black leather pouch fell from the box and landed with a soft *thunk* on the braided rug. I set the jewelry box on the dresser where it belonged, then reached down to retrieve the little bag that had fallen.

"Wait!"

I slapped my palm to my chest and was back to tongue choking. "Aunt Sylvia, don't *do* that."

Like I said, the woman had a healthy set of lungs.

"I'll take that."

Before I had a chance to inhale another breath, she snatched the pouch from the ground then tucked it into her sweater pocket.

I crossed my arms. "Look, I don't want you to think I'm being pushy or nosy or whatever. But I was hoping to spend some time this afternoon going through photos so I can pencil in some info on the back about the images. I don't know who half those people are." I gestured to the living room. "Especially Joshua 1879. Maybe you don't know him either, but I'd at least like to find out what you know about the origins of the photos, and anything you can tell me about the cabin. We've never really discussed anything like that in detail."

I gave her a smile as I led her from the room. "You know how I am with the history of things. In all the years I've been coming here, I never knew there was a sexy lumberjack who made up the history of this property."

Aunt Sylvia wrenched her arm away, frowning as she took her seat. She tugged the blanket back around her shoulders.

"You'd better be careful what you say, young lady. I wouldn't start up with any sexy talk about complete strangers."

I laughed, thinking she was joking, but stopped mid-chortle when it was clear she wasn't. I sat in the rocker across from her again. Aunt Sylvia was funny, sarcastic, loving and a real straight shooter. This cryptic and cautious creature was not the aunt I was accustomed to interacting with.

"Hey, I'm sorry." So far, she didn't seem too interested in revealing all, so I decided I should probably back off for now. "Why don't I make us some tea, then you can tell me about some of our family pics. I noticed you have a lot from the camping trips we used to go on as kids."

"You don't have to leave?"

The hopeful note in her voice was clear. Whatever tension that had arisen over the pictures and the mysterious jewelry pouch seemed to have passed. What I heard now was my aunt's unarticulated plea that I stay with her a while longer.

I was more than happy to oblige. There would be plenty of time in the future to ask her more questions about Joshua 1879.

A *year later...*

ANA EYED me as if I'd lost my mind, then shoved another forkful of salad into her mouth. She was probably spot on in wondering if I'd bought a first-class ticket for a one-way trip on crazy train. But something about the letter from my aunt's estate attorney had struck a distant chord in my soul.

After learning that Aunt Sylvia had left me her home, I'd been pondering whether to sell my aunt's beloved cabin. The news of my inheritance was akin to the universe grabbing me by the throat and giving me a vigorous shake. Suddenly, I knew what to do.

I was moving to Squirrel Cove.

After all, what could it hurt to give a new town a try? To live in my aunt's little cabin? Part of my reasoning was the ache in the pit of my stomach over the prospect of selling off the best of my childhood memories. Plus, at least if I lived in the cozy cottage, there would be a touch of the familiar to my new abode instead of renting some sterile, I-was-dumped-by-my-husband apartment.

Sure, where my aunt had lived was over a hundred miles from where I was born and raised. And yeah, it was in a small town in the mountains and the cabin gave new meaning to the word tiny. Cities were cool and everything but...

I've got nothing. Stupid cities and their interesting shit to do. Whatever.

I cleared my throat then took a sip of my chai iced tea, glancing around my favorite block on Melrose in the Fairfax District. Ana and I had been coming to this café for years, and I couldn't imagine not being able to just ring her up and say, hey! Meet me down at Chez Rendezvous for a gluten-free muffin with flax seed sprinkles.

Okay, so in reality I always ordered the triple fudge lava brownie. Quit judging me.

Anyway, hanging out at the trendy Melrose Café, sitting outside under the umbrellas, gossiping—I mean, chatting—while absorbing the scenery, that had always been our little treat to ourselves. Our way of feeling like we weren't the poor relations of L.A.—even if we kind of were.

In Los Angeles, the prices were so out of control that an average family home could easily cost a million bucks. If Vince hadn't gotten a decent job right out of college, and we hadn't been so OCD about saving for a house, we'd be lucky to have a studio apartment at this point.

I sighed. We didn't have *anything* anymore because Vince was living with his exciting new girlfriend, the one who wasn't mind-numbingly boring the way I apparently was. Then there was me, getting ready to move out of the marital home now that it had been sold and the proceeds split between us.

Ana sighed louder than I had. We competed over the weirdest things. She took a sip of her own tea then finally spoke up.

"Consider this. What will you do up there all alone? There

won't be anyone to hang out with, and besides, they probably roll up the carpet at six." She rolled her eyes. "Not that there's really anyplace to *go* there."

I scowled. Didn't she realize I'd already thought of all that? "Things might stay open till seven. Maybe eight in the summer."

She smirked. "Funny. You know what I mean. Like, remember that time when our favorite nineties band did an impromptu gig on Sunset, and we rushed over to get in. You wouldn't be able to do that if you were far away in the mountains."

"I'm not moving to Mars."

Her smirk deepened, something I hadn't known was possible until that moment. "Yes. I realize that. What I'm trying to point out is that your ability to spontaneously do something amazing will be destroyed because you'll be kickin' it with the coyotes and mountain lions."

My eyes widened. "Mountain lions? There are mountain lions?"

Why had no one told me this? I didn't remember giant, fanged wild cats the times I'd visited my aunt.

Ana shrugged. "I guess? Maybe I'm getting the lions confused with the bears." Her brow creased and she tapped her chin with one finger. "Could be it's the bears I'm thinking of."

My jaw dropped. I didn't remember anything about bears either. They were supposed to be across the Interstate in—wait for it—Big Bear.

I huffed and threw my hands in the air. "Oh, well. That's different, no worries then. As long as there aren't any mountain *lions*, I shouldn't concern myself with a few enormous, killer *bears*."

Ana grinned and waggled her eyebrows. "Does that mean you'll stay?"

"Seriously?" I fell back in my chair and angrily crossed my arms. Her button-pushing skills were epic. "That was a rotten trick."

She batted her eyelashes. "I love you."

Her blue-ribbon awards in guilt trips were rather impressive as well.

"I love you too, dork. But I need..."

I frowned, pressing my lips together as I struggled to give Ana the perfect explanation for what was churning inside me. How could I put into words what I didn't understand myself? Everyone could call what I was going through a midlife crisis, but they weren't living and breathing my reality. I was the only person who knew what was right for me, and I needed to not only get onboard, but *stay* onboard with that truth.

"What is it I'm not getting?"

Ana's tone had changed from the comfortable banter we shared most of the time, to the let's-cut-the-shit-and-figure-this-out voice that signaled she was ready to truly listen.

"I need a do-over."

She nodded slowly. "You're thinking you and Vince never should've gotten married? That having a kid was a mistake?"

I gasped. "What? No! God, no. My daughter is the *best* thing that's ever happened to me, which is part of the problem. And the early years with Vince were great, but I don't want to dwell on that right now." I groaned, shaking my head. "I've wasted so many precious hours on where did we go wrong? Why didn't I see this coming and blah blah blah. Who cares? It doesn't change the outcome.

I rubbed my chin. "No, this is more about me. It's how *I* let things run off the rails. You know, life was happening around me but instead of keeping my dreams alive, I sort of drifted down the stream, let the circumstances around me take over and distract me."

"Sort of like salmon spawning before the bears eat them alive."

I narrowed my eyes. "Enough with the bears already."

Ana noisily finished the last of her tea then pushed the glass aside. "Okay. Let's take a gander at your situation. Husband of twenty years kicks you to the curb on your anniversary because he's reached the conclusion that you're too boring to share the rest of his life with."

I massaged my temples. I wasn't sure how this was helping, but I held in the snappy comeback in case she said something less soul-destroying.

"Yes," I responded. "Carry on."

"Then, he suddenly moves in with a hot model ten years his junior who he claims he didn't meet until five minutes after you were dumped. However, this whole time, for years and years and years and—"

"Yes!"

All the heads belonging to the patio patrons whipped around and I realized I might've blurted a bit too loud. I offered my audience a tight smile, then folded my hands on the wrought iron table, leaning forward and keeping my voice low as I continued.

"Yes, I'm fully aware of all those facts. My point is, what now? Why not just go to the mountains, get away from all this crap—present company excluded—and start over? Hailey moved in with her boyfriend and has a ton of friends she hangs out with. When she still lived with us, I could barely see the blur rushing past me as she flitted from one social engagement to the next." I rolled my eyes. "And if you think Squirrel Cove is far away, what would happen to our good times together if I ended up in Florida with my folks?"

I flopped back in the chair again, then raked my fingers through my hair. The French tip nails I'd been talked into getting by Ana caught in the unruly strands that ended at my shoulders. What followed was a humiliating attempt to break loose from the brown prison of curls that I should've pinned up the way I typically did.

"The problem is—" I wrestled my hand free. "I can't remember what I wanted to be when I grew up. Like I said, I don't regret Hailey, not by a long shot. But now that she's off doing her thing, starting her own life..." I shrugged. "That's as it should be. I mean, I'm proud she has goals and interests." I let out another self-pitying sigh. "Too bad I don't."

"I call bullshit," Ana growled. "I've known you since our junior year in high school. You were in five different clubs, a cheerleader, you won that..." She frowned. "Some award—"

"The Future Historians of America."

She tilted her head. "Future Historians. How does that work? I always wondered about that."

Rubbing my forehead wasn't helping. I needed a Tylenol. "Never mind. Continue. Tell me some more about how I peaked in high school."

Ana jabbed her finger at me. "Enough. You need to be reminded that you've always had plenty of interests, skills, talents —you were a real go-getter."

I slumped in the chair and polished off my own tea. "That's the problem. Was. I *was* a go-getter."

Ana grabbed my arm. "Then go back and explore those interests again. Give yourself a chance to see where they might lead you." She released me then averted her gaze. "I suppose the money from the house and the alimony from Vince can keep you going for a while." She lifted one shoulder in a small shrug. "You know, since you already have a place to stay because you've inherited your aunt's place and all."

I arched my eyebrows. "Seriously? You mean that?"

Ana met my gaze. "I'm not *that* selfish. Pretty selfish, but not enough to doom you to try and scrape by in L.A. now that you've been so heartlessly dumped."

For a minute, I'd thought she was going to make me weepy before she squashed the warm fuzzies with the reminder of how discardable I was.

"Uh, thanks?"

I swiped the back of my hand across my forehead. It was still early spring, but the sun creeping past our personal patio umbrella was making me sweaty. Or perhaps it was early-onset menopause. With everything else slamming into me at once, why not that as well?

I regarded Ana with a frown. "Can menopause start at forty-two?"

Ana's eyes widened. "Yikes. I hope not. I don't have time for that right now. Next year, maybe." She tucked her jet-black hair behind her ears. "Actually, that director I'm working with now said that if the series we're doing doesn't get renewed, he wants me for another project he's eyeing."

Only Ana would consider a natural function of her body something that should be scheduled in her planner. But I wasn't going to miss out on this ideal opportunity to get the subject veered in her direction and away from me and my pitiful circumstances.

"How's that series been working out? Are you still having problems with the boy diva?"

I'd always been secretly jealous of Ana's career. She got to work at one of the big studios doing make-up and shared plenty of great stories whenever we had one of our café days.

"Dirk?" She rolled her eyes. "He always makes sure to wear a stretch T-shirt a couple sizes too small to display the six-pack and to highlight the gun show."

I snickered. "Is there a reason ghosthunters need to be so fit?"

"They do if they want a panting female—and male—fan base to help keep the ratings high."

I'd never been one to watch those ghost investigation or psychic wonders of the world kinds of shows, I didn't believe in that stuff. But if Real Ghostly Encounters kept my girl employed, I was all for it.

"Are you getting a chance to do some of the ghoul make-up now as well?"

The only thing I'd enjoyed about the few episodes I'd watched for Ana's sake, were the cheesy reenactments. A hearty belly laugh was guaranteed every time.

She grinned. "Yeah. In a startling development, I'm starting to enjoy working on this series a lot. As annoying and as full of himself as Dirk is, I hope it doesn't get cancelled."

"I thought it was super popular. It's been around for what, five or so years now?"

Ana nodded. "It has, but there are so many of those kinds of shows, so there's a lot of pressure on him and his team to capture amazing phenomena. In some ways, I feel bad for the guy."

"He's not getting enough action?"

She pursed her lips. "Funny. No, it's the producers. Sometimes they nix a location that Dirk is sure is a winner, because they feel the budget will be too high, or it's in an inconvenient spot or whatever." She glanced around then leaned in, lowering her voice. "And even though Dirk is a dick—" she paused to chuckle at her own joke "—his lead investigator is a true asshole. It's been pretty obvious for a while that he's jealous of Dirk's popularity. When the show started, it was about the two of them as partners, and the rest of the team answered to them. Now it's like it's all about Dirk, and Stan has been relegated to the background."

"Damn. Whenever you tell me these behind-the-scenes stories, it's like what's going on behind the camera is way more interesting than what they film."

"Right?" She grinned. "I mean, I already love my job, but all the drama on set is the icing on the cake."

"Yeah. Totally."

I gave a shaky laugh. This envy thing had to stop. She was my best friend in the whole world, and it wasn't her fault that she hadn't let her husband discourage her from pursuing her dreams.

Ana had stayed on her path. Instead, I'd taken whatever job came along to pay half of the mortgage the way Vince insisted I do.

Not that I couldn't have continued pursuing my interests during my off hours, but giving in to the subtle pressure to be a part of what *he* enjoyed, then raising our daughter he rarely had time for because of *his* career—I'd allowed any smidgen of excitement about my interests dwindle away until...

I became boring. Boring, boring, boring.

"Okay," I announced. "I'm over it."

"Huh?" Ana crumpled her napkin on top of her salad remnants and was eyeing the check. "Over what?"

"My whining."

She tapped a finger to her lips as if in deep thought. "Hmm. It's only been about three months since the axe fell. I'd give yourself another month, maybe two, before you quit complaining all the time."

"I complain all the time?"

"Well, only most of it."

Great. A boring whiner. What a winning combination.

"Then that settles it," I announced with determination. "From now on, the past is the past. I'm moving to my aunt's cabin in Squirrel Cove and beginning a whole new life." I furrowed my brow. "Theme of new life to be determined at a later date." I pressed my lips together. "But not too much later."

Ana offered me a smile, one that indicated she approved. "I'll hold you to that."

My chest tightened. I was really doing this. I was going to a place where I wouldn't know anyone, where it would be up to me to decide what happened next. No husband to answer to, no daughter to take into consideration before making a decision.

I met Ana's eyes. "You promise?"

"Hell yes. No more Mrs. Nice Bestie."

I could've pointed out that her harsh assessment of my circumstances hadn't been what any sane person would consider nice, but I'd be wrong. Her words were exactly what I needed to get me off my starting-to-sag behind and begin anew. My own smile stretched wide.

"Good. Now let's get outta here. I need to shop for moving boxes."

CHAPTER

TWO

"Oh my God, Mom. Why the hell did you bring this piece of junk with you?" Hailey shook her head. "You know you can get a brand-new toaster for about twenty bucks, right? I bet you can even find one that won't blacken one side of the bread and leave the other completely untoasted."

I yanked the box of random kitchen items from her, the contents clattering together. "It still has life left in it. I need to be frugal until I have a better idea of what my future holds."

She snorted. "I can tell you what your future holds. Funky, inedible toast."

I dropped the box onto the small sofa in the main room of my aunt's cabin, next to her old chair with the rainbow-colored Afghan draped over it. *No, wait.* My eyes burned. It was my cabin now. Thinking of her home as belonging to me was tough. I kept expecting to see Aunt Sylvia emerging from around the corner or croaking out my name if she needed help with something.

I'd give anything to hear her voice again.

Hailey touched my arm. "Mom, are you okay?"

I gave myself a mental shake. "Yeah. Totally fine." I cleared the emotion from my throat. "I think once we get the microwave and spice rack from your truck, we should be good." I regarded her with a feeble smile. "Then we can grab a late lunch."

Frankly, I was exhausted. As far as I was concerned, all my crap could stay in boxes until I felt like dealing with it. It wasn't as if the queen would be visiting anytime soon. I grunted to myself. And after Hailey went home the next day, probably not anyone else, either.

I glanced up and noted Hailey peering through the contents of the built-in cedar cabinet located next to the fireplace.

"This is cool, Mom. I never paid much attention to the details of this place when I used to visit."

She tugged on the top drawer below the closet, the twisted branch handle one of the many fanciful touches to the cabin. It didn't easily give in to her efforts, and I was reminded how the solid wood home would need a lot of tender loving care. I doubted my aunt had done much in the way of maintenance in recent years.

"Well," I chuckled. "Home features aren't exactly a priority to a kid. Now that you're living in your own place, you'll start noticing all kinds of things you never gave a second thought to when you were younger."

I sniffed. Now I was fighting back tears over my daughter having left the nest. I couldn't wait to find out what dagger to the chest was next on the ruining-Cate's-day list.

Hailey was bent over the now-open drawer with her back to me. "Very true. Ooh, what's this?"

She twisted around then straightened, holding up the very pouch Aunt Sylvia had stuffed into her pocket the last time I ever saw her.

"Give me that."

I snatched the item from my startled daughter's hand then wondered what the hell was wrong with me. I'd rather surprised myself as well.

"Sorry." I winced. "I don't know why I did that."

Hailey crossed her arms, a frown marring her brow. "Watch the grabby hands, Mom. Sheesh."

I gave her an embarrassed smile, then considered the black, butter-soft leather bag, the weight of whatever was inside heavier than I'd expected. Because my aunt had been so petite, I couldn't imagine her wearing whatever type of jewelry there was inside. I drew my eyebrows together. Maybe it wasn't jewelry at all.

"Well?" Hailey huffed. "Are you going to stare at it all day, or see what's inside?"

I narrowed my eyes at her. "Watch your tone, Miss Smarty Pants."

She shrugged. "Fair enough. But you're the one who yanked that thing from me as if it were a snake. You've got me dying of curiosity! Not cool, Mom. Not cool."

Ah, my little drama queen. Some things never changed. "All right, but let's sit down. My feet are killing me."

Hailey grabbed my box of kitchen accessories, then tossed it off the couch before plopping down and taking its place. I pinched the bridge of my nose at the hearty clanging of the contents as the box hit the rug. She'd pretty much guaranteed I'd need that new toaster after all.

Hailey patted the other cushion. "Come on, hurry up. Maybe Aunt Sylvia picked up a rare jewel or a gold doubloon on one of her adventures."

I took a seat next to my wildly imaginative daughter. "A *doubloon*? Where did that come from?"

"She took all those Caribbean cruises. Duh."

"Dear lord," I muttered, but couldn't deny I was filled with curiosity, too. Ever since the day Aunt Sylvia basically did to me what I'd just done to my daughter, I'd wanted to know what mysterious item she was hiding in the bag.

Hailey leaned in, her nose almost in my lap as I carefully undid the ties of the pouch. I fumbled with the silk cords, then opened the little bag. The first thing my fingers made contact with was a chain, so I pulled it out, the gold links dragging a heavier disc along with it.

"Ooh..." Hailey breathed out. "How beautiful."

The thick, flat gold pendant rested in my palm, the attached chain falling between my fingers. I tested the weight of the plum-sized disc, wondering if it was perhaps real gold. If so, it would be quite valuable. Maybe that's why Aunt Sylvia had been so protective of the necklace?

At the same time, why would she be so secretive about it with me? She'd shown me where all her important papers were, had entrusted me with a list of her passwords to her accounts as well as giving me the spare key to her safety deposit box. Why would she then hide the existence of a piece of jewelry?

"Very odd," I mumbled to myself.

"Not really." Hailey traced the engraving on the front of the pendant with her forefinger. "It's an infinity sign. Many cultures throughout history have used this symbol to represent everlasting life, love or even chaos." She brushed her thumb over the surface. "Hmm. It's interesting that it's deeply engraved in the gold. That's very significant to alchemists. I wonder if it's real?"

I shook my head, raising my eyebrows. "Not sure about the alchemist or gold thing. But that's not what I meant when I said it was odd. I'm familiar with what an infinity sign is. I'm just trying to figure out why Sylvia had it in that drawer instead of her jewelry box."

I shuddered at the memory of that night when the box fell from her dresser for no discernible reason.

Hailey gave a sharp nod. "Let's check the drawer for clues."

I snorted. "Lead the way, Nancy Drew."

She gave me a smirk. "You're hilarious."

I smirked back. "Aren't I, though?"

The second I glanced down at the contents of the drawer, my heart jumped into my throat. *The old photos.* Why did she move them out of the box they'd been in? I couldn't deny that my *actual* first thought wasn't a generic memory of a bunch of pictures. No. One picture jumped into my head, an image that had been randomly popping into my thoughts ever since that day a year ago when I'd first seen it.

Joshua 1879.

My mouth went dry, and I licked my lips. I reached for the ribbon-tied photos at the same time my daughter did, although, my fingers trembled while hers remained steady. At this point, she probably thought I was cracking around the edges.

She might be right.

I lifted the pile from the drawer before she could grab them, my hands still shaking. I don't know why, but I was desperate to see that picture again, to see *him*.

"Maybe we should wait and do all this after lunch, Mom. You don't look so good."

Hailey's concerned tone brought me back to reality. I glanced up and was met with her worried expression.

"No, that's all right, I'm fine. Unless you're hungry?"

Hailey tilted her head. "You know, I kind of am. We've been going non-stop for hours. And this way, we can take our time and go through them when we come back." She grinned. "I bet there's some other cool stuff in there, too. Aunt Sylvia was amazing."

I nodded. "You're right. I got excited about finding these, I guess." I gave her a smile. "I've seen them before and you're correct. They're very cool."

I made a mental note to go to the history museum down in Stagecoach in the coming week. The fact that I'd never followed through when I originally saw the pics irritated me for some reason.

After putting the photos away, my attention was drawn back to the pendant. Something about leaving the unusual medallion with the pictures made me uneasy. Now that I'd discovered it, I couldn't bear to parted with the necklace for one second. On the other hand, it seemed a bit over the top to wear such a dramatic item to lunch. I wrapped my fingers around the pouch then decided to drop it into my purse.

Glancing sideways, I noted that Hailey was busily gathering her phone, keys, stainless steel water bottle, lip gloss and whatever else it was she carried around with her, then dumping everything into her large Boho style bag. She didn't seem to have noticed me tuck the pendant away into my own, more compact cross-body purse.

Why I cared whether she saw me or not, I couldn't imagine. I yanked my ponytail tighter and decided to take a rest from obsessing over the necklace. It clearly meant a lot to my aunt, and for that reason alone I'd take good care of it.

With a grunt, Hailey hoisted the stuffed fabric bag over her shoulder then straightened, blowing out a puff of air that made her bangs lift from her forehead for a second before falling again. She regarded me.

"Okay. Ready."

I chuckled. "You sure? You might've forgotten something."

"There you go being hilarious again, Mom. True comedienne."

Once we decided on the cute French bistro where I used to take Aunt Sylvia to when she was still going out and about—that just so happened to have an amazing variety of fresh baked desserts— we jumped into my beat-up, fifteen-year-old sedan and headed into the small town. My ex had determined that he should keep the Lincoln Navigator because he had a 'real' job and needed to appear professional.

Whatever.

The tourists weren't in full force yet since it was still early spring, so we were able to find a nearby parking spot without any trouble. As I opened my door, it made an ungodly groaning noise, announcing my arrival to the peaceful village that was surrounded by majestic pine trees, quaint boutiques, homey restaurants and a giant carved wood lumberjack in the town's square.

I snapped to attention as I stared at it. I'd never noticed it all that much before. The aging statue had been there since my childhood, a symbol of the town's history. The carving was simply a part of the landscape, something that had faded into the back of my mind over the years.

Until now.

Now, anything and everything related to lumberjacks would pique my interest. Which was slightly goofy, but I couldn't stop thinking about Joshua 1879. Maybe when I went through all of Sylvia's things, I'd discover something more about him and his story. Then there was the museum I should've visited a long time ago...

"Mom! Starving over here."

My head snapped around. "Huh?"

She rolled her eyes as she jerked a thumb over her shoulder. "I wanna get in there before they sell out of the lemon tarts."

Someone had a good memory when it came to sweets. They'd always been a favorite of hers, something she'd order whenever we visited Aunt Sylvia.

We made our way inside, the little café empty except for one elderly couple who seemed about ready to leave. Crumpled napkins and espresso cups were all that remained on the round, white wrought iron table where they sat.

"Can we eat outside on the patio?"

Hailey regarded me with childlike excitement, my stomach clenching as I recalled her kid self standing in this very spot. Now, she was grown up and gone—along with my marriage. I swallowed hard. Not that I hadn't already given the subject of my solo existence plenty of thought, but for whatever reason, the harsh truth of my new reality slammed into me.

I cleared my throat. "Yeah, of course."

The hostess greeted us then led the way outside, a cool breeze making me wish I'd brought a sweater or something to go over my sweatshirt. I was such a wimp when it came to the cold. Probably all those years living in the scorching desert of Los Angeles had forever altered my body chemistry.

Hailey regarded her menu with serious intent, her eyebrows pinched together, and forehead creased. For my part, I was in the process of resisting the urge to order everything. I hadn't realized how hungry I was until we arrived.

She placed her menu on the table with an air of finality. "I'm getting the cranberry walnut salad."

I arched my eyebrows. "That's it? I thought you were starving."

Hailey patted her flat tummy. "I need to save room for the awesome breadbasket and lemon tart."

I sighed as I glanced down at all the food choices, scraping my teeth across my bottom lip. Would the server think it strange if I ordered an éclair for lunch and the triple fudge cake for dessert? Lately, chocolate and wine were all I felt like ingesting.

"I guess I'll have the salad, too." I closed the menu and shoved it to the edge of the table.

Hailey blinked at me several times. "You hate salad. Especially when it contains fruit and nuts."

I chuckled shakily. "That's not true. Who doesn't love dried up bits of fruit on a bed of jungle lettuce?"

Hailey heaved out a sigh. "Mom. For real. It's been a rough few days packing and a long day dragging all those boxes in and out of the cars. Have a damn sandwich."

"I should start watching what I eat more." I picked at the edge of the menu as if it might give me a sign, a signal that it was okay to eat something with melted cheese or lots of mayo. "I'm not getting any younger, you know."

Hailey smacked her forehead. "Seriously. Stop. I bet if Ana was here, she'd be telling you to *relax* and quit freaking out over what to order for lunch."

I frowned. "I'm not freaking out. It's just..."

I didn't want to confess to my daughter that ever since her father began dating the supermodel, I'd become bizarrely self-conscious about my weight. Over the course of our marriage, I hadn't put on more than fifteen or twenty pounds, but after seeing the rail thin Gia he was madly in love with, I realized there was about a forty-pound difference between us. Not gonna lie—the realization was a punch to the gut.

"The hell with it. I'll get the crab melt."

Hailey grinned. "That's the spirit. Maybe I'll get one, too."

With that major decision out of the way, we sat back to enjoy our brief break from the day's chores and basked in the pleasant afternoon. A group of squawking blue jays took up a loud chorus nearby, their song of protest eliciting a potent memory of Squirrel Cove. Everything about what was now my new home—the birds, the chattering squirrels, the continuous mountain breeze, soothing scent of pine—it was all a balm to my aching soul.

Never mind lunch, my move to the mountains was the true major decision. I smiled to myself. For once, I felt as if I'd made the right one.

THREE

"I'm going to explode." Hailey filled her cheeks with air as if to illustrate they were about to burst.

"Yeah..." I longed for the sweatpants I'd almost chosen to wear, instead of the jeans that suddenly felt as though they were one size smaller than they were before lunch. "Maybe we should walk around a bit, browse in some shops."

Or take a nap.

"Ooh, good idea. We should totally go into that metaphysical gift shop here. I love that place."

I signed the receipt then tucked my debit card back into my wallet. "When have you ever been in there?" I wasn't aware she was interested in such things, and *I'd* certainly never taken her into Guinevere's Garden before.

"The last time I visited, when Maggie came with us? Remember, we walked into town and hung out all day while you were getting Aunt Sylvia set up with the home care people?"

"Oh, right. Wow. That was almost three years ago. I forgot."

Hailey had been between her junior and senior year of high school and bored out of her mind. I'd suggested she bring her bestie with her to spend the week in the mountains. We'd stayed in a motel closer to town that boasted a pool, then while they explored or swam, I helped Sylvia.

"Sure. We can do that. I also want to check out the herbal tea shop."

Hailey scooted back her chair, the metal legs scraping on the concrete. "Cool. Maybe I'll get a psychic reading while I'm there."

I barked out a laugh. "Oh my God, Hailey. Don't waste your money on that nonsense."

She crossed her arms with a scowl. "What do you mean, nonsense?"

I gaped at her as if she'd grown another head. "I'm just saying... psychics and all that mystical stuff isn't real. It's only wishful thinking on the part of people who are searching for a shortcut to the answers in life." I rose from my chair, shaking my head in wonder. "When did you start getting into that sort of thing? You never mentioned anything to me about spooky stuff."

Not that I'd nosed around in her private space when she was living at home, but I wasn't completely oblivious to what was in her bedroom. I'd never noticed pentagrams or crystal balls on display.

Hailey held up one of the collection of pendants she wore around her neck. "Why do you think I wear this?"

I leaned in, examining the purple crystal point. "I don't know. It's pretty?"

"Yes, but it's also an ametrine crystal. Very spiritual, and quite cleansing."

"Ametrine? You mean amethyst, right?"

She huffed as if I were a complete idiot. "No. *Ametrine.* It's a combination of amethyst and citrine. It's an excellent stone to restore balance and focus in your life. And of course, it contains other properties if you want to really work with it on a deeper level."

"Oh. I didn't know that." *Still think it's baloney.*

Hailey dropped the crystal from her fingers then showed me a medallion-like, bronze disc with a lined symbol etched in it. I couldn't help but be reminded of the pendant in my purse, but this was much smaller and not as bright.

"This is a rune. This particular one represents insight and inspiration. I never take it off."

She regarded me with great seriousness and keeping a straight face was bordering on the painful. However, I wouldn't hurt my girl's feelings for all the money in the world. She had the right to her own beliefs, even if I didn't share them.

I nodded sagely. "Oh yeah. I've heard of runes."

Hailey smirked at me. "You think I'm full of crap, don't you?"

I gasped, slapping a hand to my chest to help add a dramatic flair. "I'd never think that about you!"

She rolled her eyes. "Mom...we don't have to agree on every-thing. Just don't make fun of me, okay?"

This time her expression radiated insecurity and it tugged at my heart.

"Of course not, sweetie. I'd never make fun of you." My smile was genuine as I placed a soft hand on her arm. "If I've ever made you feel that way, I'm sorry. I promise it wasn't intentional."

Hailey shook her head. "No, not you." She winced. "Dad."

Oh boy. The triangular dynamic of exes and a shared adult daughter who loved us both was brutal. I'd kept all my personal seething rage and severe hurt from her the best that I could. I'm sure I slipped up here and there, and she wasn't an idiot. There were times I know I wasn't at my best around her. However, I worked hard at keeping negative comments about her father out of our conversations and I'd never brought up any of my issues with him or the divorce.

"Well..." I shifted from foot to foot, shoving to the back of my mind all the inappropriate jabs I wanted to toss out. "Maybe you misunderstood what he said. I'm sure he didn't mean to mock your beliefs."

She huffed. "Uh, I'm thinking 'you don't actually believe that crap is real, do you?' and 'I thought we raised you to be smarter than that', isn't too difficult to interpret. Not sure I can imagine it being taken a different way."

"Oh." *Dammit, Vince.* I scoured my brain for the appropriate response to that morsel of info. "Well, maybe you should talk to him about it, tell him how it made you feel."

Hailey bit her bottom lip. "Mom, you're the best. I shouldn't have said anything. I didn't mean to put you in the middle of our conflict."

I sighed. "Hey. Don't worry about me. Say whatever you want. Your parents' divorce isn't your fault and it's not your responsibility to censor your conversation to please us."

Hailey shrugged. "I never thought it was my fault. It was more me blaming myself that you guys stayed together so long. You know, because of what Dad said."

I tilted my head, willing my eyes not to start twitching. "Oh? What did he say?"

She brushed the air with one hand. "Oh, nothing that I hadn't already figured out a long time ago. Just that you guys stayed together until I was out of the house, so it wouldn't affect me and all that."

I laughed shakily. "Oh right. That."

I must have missed the 'we're staying together for the sake of the kid' memo. It sure would've been nice if someone had bothered to share with me that my marriage was on a timer that was slowly running out.

I snatched up my purse from the back of my chair. "Well, might as well get moving. Who knows how long the shops will stay open?" I slung the strap over my shoulder. "Guinevere's Garden?"

"Yup." She grinned, jumping up from her chair then looping

33

her arm through mine. "I can show you all the different stones and symbols, explain what they all mean."

Oh goody.

"Sure. Sounds cool."

Truth was, I'd do anything for her.

STROLLING along the narrow aisles of Guinevere's Garden, huffing incense and gaping at the ridiculous prices for the metaphysical bits and baubles, I silently willed Hailey to become as bored as I was so we could leave. Since she seemed to be in her element and giddy with joy, I didn't think that was likely.

Maybe I could faint. *Or knock something over.* The embarrassment factor would probably encourage her to make a hasty retreat. I squinched up my nose. I couldn't really afford to randomly smash overpriced junk simply because I was bored out of my skull.

The sigh I let out was loud enough that it drew the attention of a few patrons also strolling along, as well as a scowl from my daughter. I'd thought for sure the strains of whale cries and tinkling chimes playing over the sound system would've drowned me out.

Over by the register, I spotted a long glass display case containing jewelry and other small objects. At least jewelry was something I could understand. I didn't care about its supposed hidden meaning as long as it was nice to look at.

When I reached the case, I peered down at the first section, each of the three shelves covered in velvet trays stuffed with a wild variety of rings. Most were silver, although a few gold ones were included. Some were only metal work with symbols I vaguely recognized or animals and other creatures. Wolves, dolphins, dragonflies and fairies were among the designs.

Of course, a large majority of the styles were decorated with stones. Some of the gems were cut, but I had no idea how authentic they were. Somehow, I doubted there were diamonds and rubies among the selections, but hey, considering the price tags on them, I could be wrong. Then there were other stones that were polished or seemed to be in their natural state. Those were more reminiscent of the ones my daughter wore.

I sauntered over to the next section and my stomach tightened. *Pendants.* In many ways, the pendants were similar in design to the rings. But what drew my gaze were the ones that were more like medallions—more like the necklace from my aunt that was currently residing in my purse. Had she purchased it from this store?

"See something that calls to you?"

I glanced up at the sound of the whiskey-tinged voice, the woman the voice belonged to leaning against the counter on one elbow and regarding me with a lopsided grin. She wore a flowing white shirt with bell sleeves over a pair of brown, leather leggings that disappeared into a pair of worn, black suede boots. The heels of the boots were flat, but the leather of the boots rose to just below her knees. A loose, green sash with a variety of silk knots interwoven in an intricate design was tied loosely around her waist.

Between her ensemble and shoulder length, tightly coiled auburn hair, I wouldn't have batted an eyelash if she'd said 'Aargh, ahoy me matey'.

"Oh, uh..." I let my eyes drift back to the selection below me. "Well, that round one with the pointy star looks interesting."

I pointed in the general direction of a bronze pendant with a pentagram on it. Not much like the one I had, but similar in size and it wasn't set with any stones like the others that were for sale.

"Nice choice." She stepped behind the counter, inching her way between the display case and the ornately carved wood podium on which the register was perched. "Are you wiccan, or still feeling your way around things?" She chuckled as she opened up the case.

"Maybe it's a gift for a metaphysically-minded friend? No offense, but I'm not picking up any mystical vibes from you at all." She glanced up before reaching for the medallion. "In truth, you seem rather closed off."

Great. Free insults with every purchase. "Look," I chuckled in a blasé tone. "I'm not into all this stuff. If that's being closed off, so be it."

She straightened, her green eyes boring into me. A spark danced up my spine and for a second, it felt as if I couldn't swallow. A breath was pushed out of me then the strange moment passed.

"I don't think this is what you're looking for, Cate." She offered me the pendant. "But take a gander if you like."

"Oh, I was just—" I jerked back my hand before accepting the piece of jewelry from her. "Wait. How did you know my name?"

She shrugged. "Let's just say there's a reason I charge for my services."

I arched my eyebrows. "Dare I ask what services you provide?"

"Go on, Cate. Ask." She winked. "Live on the edge."

I found myself growing somewhat fond of this odd woman who was being overly familiar despite the fact we were strangers. I held out my hand.

"All right. But before you divulge your superpower, we should be properly introduced. As you inexplicably manage to know already, I'm Cate. And you are?"

She grasped my hand and the spark returned with an additional vibration where our palms joined. "I'm Viv, owner and resident psychic of Guinevere's Garden."

"Awesome!" Hailey burst into view next to Viv as if she'd materialized from thin air. "Are you available to do a reading this afternoon? I'd love to have one if you are."

My eyes rolled before I could stop them, and I released Viv's hand. I regarded my daughter who was glaring at me as if I'd kicked a puppy.

"Unfortunately..." I chuckled as if I hadn't just silently mocked the shop owner standing in front of me. "We have so much to do today. You see, I'm in the process of moving into my great aunt's cabin, so..." I swallowed hard, my confidence waning under the judgmental gaze of Hailey and Viv. "Super busy and all that."

"Uh-huh," Viv commented before turning her attention to Hailey. "Let me give my assistant a heads up, then we can go to the back for a reading."

"W-wait." I held up a finger, but Viv was already sauntering away. I huffed and turned to Hailey. "I wasn't making an excuse. We actually *are* super busy."

She slammed her fists on her hips. "Except for the part where you were saying you wanted to go to the tea shop and the candy store after this. What does *that* have to do with moving?"

I crossed my arms back at her. "Yeah... Well... I need supplies for my new home."

Hailey snorted. "Tea and candy?"

"Yes." I averted my gaze. "Absolute essentials."

Hailey grasped my arm. "Please? I'll do a short one." She gasped. "Oh my God. You should totally do one, too!"

My jaw dropped. "Not in a zillion years."

"But, *Mom...*"

I pinched the bridge of my nose. "Nope, nope and nope. But you go ahead, honey. The tea shop is just a few doors down. I can go wander around while you get your reading done."

Viv sidled up to Hailey, grinning at me. "Tsk, tsk, Cate. You don't know what you're missing."

"Oh, I'll just have to learn to go through life without getting my palm read or...whatever."

I was so out of my element. The only knowledge of the supernatural that I possessed was from the occasional movie that featured spooky subject matter, but it wasn't something I sought out. As for books, I read mystery novels and all the characters in those books were boring ol' human beings with no magical abilities.

"Your loss, kiddo." Viv slapped the side of my shoulder as if we were old pals. "Still want to take a peek at this pendant?"

She held up her hand, the pentagram dangling from her fingers, hanging from a leather cord.

"Wow, Mom." Hailey regarded me with a shocked expression. "Are you starting to get into Wiccan stuff?"

"No, I was simply...curious."

Hailey nodded. "Ooh, is it because of Aunt Sylvia's pendant?"

I needed to get out of there. Something about Viv being aware of the pendant's existence made me uncomfortable, and I instantly regretted not leaving it at the cabin. I placed my hand protectively over my purse. Viv's eyes tracked my movement, and I became even more uneasy.

"No, not at all." I laughed shakily. "Just killing time while you shopped."

Hailey's face fell. "Oh."

I donned the sincerest smile I could manage. "Welp. You two have fun." I wasn't about to set foot back in that shop again. "Text me when you're done, and I'll tell you where I am."

"Or you could come back and meet her here in about thirty minutes." Viv's grin bordered on the maniacal. Clearly, she was aware of my discomfort and wasn't above rubbing my nose in it.

"That's all right." I smirked. "I have a ton of tea shopping to do. Could take a while."

Viv threw back her head and let out a loud cackle as Hailey poked me in the ribs. I frowned at Hailey.

"As I was *saying*, you two have fun and I'll see you later."

Before either of them could add any more commentary, I briskly made my way down an empty aisle, side-stepping a couple entering the store and emerged into the fresh air of freedom. Something nagged at me, an inner compulsion to go back inside and go through with the reading after all, but I shook it off. No point in allowing myself to be sucked into a bunch of nonsense in a bid to make myself feel better.

I clutched my purse to my body. As soon as I got back to the cabin, I'd put the pendant away somewhere safe and forget all about it.

FOUR

"Sounds like you're settling in okay," said Ana, her words barely discernible through the noise of hearty chewing.

"Yeah, pretty much." I cradled my cell between shoulder and ear as I emptied the remaining books from the final box of my move.

"How long did Hailey stay?"

Not long enough. "She left yesterday."

"Oh wow. Only a couple days, huh? That sucks."

I resisted the urge to sigh in agreement, kicking the empty box aside before dropping into the overstuffed chair that used to be Aunt Sylvia's favorite and had become mine as well.

"It's all right. She has work, school..." *A life.*

"So, tell the truth. On a scale of one to ten, what's the boredom level?"

I wouldn't give her the satisfaction of answering with 'eleven', so I chose a half-truth instead. "Well, it's not as if I don't have plenty to do at the house. Aunt Sylvia didn't really keep up with maintenance, and I can see I'll have a lot of projects ahead of me."

"Maybe you can find yourself a hot and hunky carpenter to keep you warm for when the snows arrive."

I was treated to lip-smacking sounds but was unclear whether they were related to what she was eating or her comment.

"First off, I doubt it." I already had a sense of what the tiny town had to offer. "And second of all, not interested."

Ana snorted. "Right. Because hot and hunky carpenters are *so* repulsive."

This time, I did sigh. "That's not what I meant. It's that I'm not interested in searching for some guy to take the place of Vince. I need to figure it out for myself first, know what it is *I* want going forward. It can't be about pleasing a man or putting his needs before my own. I'm done with that."

"You don't need to marry the guy. You can still put your needs first without a relationship." She snickered. "If you know what I mean."

I groaned. "Not interested in any of *that* right now, either."

"Gasp. I wouldn't survive."

A change of subject was in order. "So, what's new with you?"

"Not much of a subtle topic segue, but I'll bite." Ana chuckled. "Well, let's see. The sixth season of Real Ghostly Encounters starts taping next week, so I'll be hard at work for a while until the season's finished. To be honest, I wasn't sure they were going to continue with the show after what happened. I was already putting feelers out just in case."

I drew my eyebrows together. "What happened?" I'd been a tad distracted lately.

"Oh man, I thought I told you. The co-investigator, Stan, was killed."

I straightened in the chair. I loved a good mystery after all. "Seriously? When? Was it murder?"

"¡Ay, caramba! You and your fascination with murders. No,

they're pretty sure it was an accident. Poor guy tumbled down a mine shaft while scouting a location."

My heart rate ticked up a notch. "But it might *not* be an accident. Maybe someone made his death *look* like an accident."

"Oh brother," Ana mumbled. "Not to sound cold blooded, but I'm just relieved I still have a job."

"That is cold blooded, Ana. Someone died."

"He wasn't exactly popular. No joke, the dude was a monumental jerk."

"Ah-ha!" I held up my pointer finger as if she could see me. "So, there are several potential suspects."

"You're possessed. Why don't you come hang out with me at the taping? Maybe get some good gossip, go all Agatha Christie on everyone. We're doing the cast promo shots along with filming a segment for the first episode that addresses how sad everyone is that Stan was killed."

"*Are* they that sad?"

"Actually, I think there was a celebration with champagne and caviar when his death was announced."

"Damn." I couldn't deny how curious the whole situation made me. "He was really despised that much?"

"Trust me, he screwed over so many people, it's ridiculous. And even though Dirk is annoying, Stan was a special kind of irritating. He was so over the top serious about the paranormal and treated us as if he was some great scientist and we were all a bunch of idiots."

Now I had to know this guy's story and what had happened to him. "Well, I suppose I could make time to hang out for a day or two."

"Nice. I have to lure you with murder and gossip so you'll come visit me."

"I haven't even been here three whole days! Cut me a break."

Ana laughed. "You're so easy to work up, Cate. I'm messing with you."

Yup. She always managed to get me. "Of course you are. I knew that."

"Then that means I can count on you next week? I have to get there at the crack of dawn, so you should probably drive out on Sunday and spend the night. Or, you could just come over now."

I frowned. "Yeah, right. I'm not driving to L.A. right *now*. It's after seven and I'm tired from unpacking. I'll see you on Sunday."

Ana let out a dramatic sigh. "I guess. But you've officially been labeled a party pooper."

We chatted a bit more, working out the logistics of my visit before hanging up. As I changed out of my work sweats and into my comfy, flannel pajamas that featured dancing blue bunnies, I tried not to let my thoughts drift to a darker place. Even though it seemed as if everyone else but me was living an exciting life, that didn't mean it was true.

As I padded the few steps across the floor from the bathroom to the kitchen, I caught some movement out of the corner of my eye. I whipped my head around to see what it was, the *thunk* of my purse sounding as it landed on the braided rug. Instead of continuing to my destination to boil water for tea, I veered into the living room instead.

I hadn't touched my purse all day and it had been in the same spot from when Hailey and I got back from our trip into town the day before. I'd set it on a side table, leaning against a hurricane glass table lamp. I retrieved my bag from the floor, frowning. It wasn't as if a strong wind had blown through, or an earthquake had struck.

My mind latched onto the day Aunt Sylvia's jewelry box had fallen, the same day that the pouch with the... *pendant*. With a shaky hand I unzipped the top of my purse and fished around for the necklace I'd forgotten to put away like I'd planned to. My fingers wrapped around the soft leather of the pouch, and once I pulled it free, I tossed my purse onto the sofa.

I considered the object in my hand, testing the weight the same way I had when I first held it. A part of me wished I'd stayed at Guinevere's Garden while Hailey had her reading. Then maybe I could've searched around the shop for other necklaces like this one without being under Viv's scrutinizing gaze.

With trembling fingers, I opened the pouch to remove the pendant. This would be the first time I had a chance to examine the necklace unobserved, without Hailey peering over my shoulder. I don't know why that mattered to me, but for some reason it did.

I shifted on my feet as I pulled the piece of jewelry from its fabric prison. A part of me felt bad for being so secretive about the pendant with Hailey, but on the other hand, she hadn't wanted to reveal anything about her reading, either. I suppose that made us even.

I held the shiny gold disc under the light of the lamp, angling it this way and that. The infinity symbol was more deeply engraved into the metal than I remembered. The sheen to the surface was also quite bright, almost as if it had been painted with a gold foil effect. I brushed my thumb across the surface, feeling the deep grooves of the engraving.

Without a thought, I opened the chain's clasp, draped the necklace around my neck then closed the link. The pendant rested on my chest, just below the collar line of my pajama top at the top of my cleavage. The feel of it was solid, almost too heavy, yet I found it to be calming at the same time.

I covered the pendant with my palm and closed my eyes, a surge of warmth passing through me. The sensation was one of comfort and safety, almost as though I'd found home. I smiled. For the first time since I could remember, it seemed like the future held promise.

I can do this. I can find who I was meant to be.

The floor behind me creaked, breaking the moment. I turned around and almost choked on my tongue, my eyes blinking rapidly as I tried to draw in air. With a gut instinct I hadn't realized I possessed, my hand shot out and grabbed the fireplace poker. I pointed it at the tall intruder, staring at me as if he was more surprised to see me than I was at seeing him.

"How did you get in here?" I demanded, with a few stabbing motions of the poker in his direction. "I'll warn you. I know advanced Tae Bo. I wouldn't come any closer!"

I could be wrong, but my wobbling voice probably wasn't inspiring much fear in the brawny He-Man who'd materialized in my living room. Mentally calculating how quickly I could hurtle over the stove and out the back door, I tried to come up with more reasons why he should get the hell out of my house, *now.*

"And, not only that, but I just sharpened this poker before you got here." I tried not to cringe. What was I even talking about? "And...I have a Life Alert necklace on, see?" I held up the pendant with the hand not stabbing the air with the poker. "One push of this symbol, and the entire SWAT team will be crashing down that door. If I were you, buster, I'd be running for my life."

With what I hoped was a menacing scowl, I continued to jab the poker in his direction as if I were in a fencing match. When he took a step forward, I lunged, and to my utter horror the poker plunged into his body. I let out a high-pitched scream then gritted my teeth, bracing myself for the blood to come spurting forth from the murderous wound I'd inflicted.

I gasped, frozen as I gaped at his un-murdered and un-bloodied form. Everything had happened in an instant, and I realized that my weapon hadn't pierced flesh. Instead, it had merely passed through his body as if he were a hologram instead of a real person. I also noted for the first time a light glow outlining his form.

The poker fell from my hand, a wave of dizziness washing over me. I pointed at him weakly, trying to draw air into my lungs to speak.

"Y-you... I..." I licked my lips, my mouth filled with cotton. "This can't be real."

Had I been drinking earlier? I couldn't remember having anything stronger than French Roast with half and half. I touched my hand to my forehead, still trying to make sense of the past few minutes. To make matters worse, my burly intruder still hadn't said a word.

I groaned. That meant I was hallucinating and had lost my entire mind. *Great.* Next, I'd be mumbling to myself while shuffling around the grocery store with the locals whispering to each other about the crazy lady living in their midst.

"I agree," said my hallucination. "I'm surprised you can see me." A cloud passed over his features. "It's been so long since anyone could."

My jaw that had been hanging open snapped shut. "What? Why wouldn't someone be able to see—" My jaw snapped shut again, and I worried I'd crack my teeth if I didn't knock it off. "Oh my God. You're Joshua1879, aren't you?"

His picture had been blurry, but I recognized the facial hair, the outfit with suspenders, the beige, short-sleeve cotton work shirt open at the collar, the muscles...

He tilted his head. "I'm Joshua, yes. Are you referring to the year I died?"

My knees gave out and I landed hard on the floor, the air rushing from my lungs with an *oomph*. Joshua dropped to his haunches in front of me, his brow furrowed in an expression of concern.

"What's wrong? Are you unwell?"

I hmphed. "Evidently *quite* unwell."

"I wish I could be more helpful, but in my current state, I can't physically interact with you." Joshua rubbed his chin. "Perhaps I could harness enough energy to bring you..." He shook his head. "No, that wouldn't work. Like I said, it's been so long since I've interacted with anyone on this plane, some of the limitations have slipped my mind."

I couldn't stop staring, wasn't sure if I should embrace the reality of what was happening in front of me or continue to pursue the theory that I'd gone nuts. Accepting that Joshua was real seemed more fun. He certainly wasn't hard to look at.

The features I hadn't been able to discern in the photo were now clear. His hair was a wavy, dark brown and on the longer side, the ends curling up a bit right below his ears. Dark lashes framed his bright green eyes, and his beard only helped add to his incredibly masculine appearance.

Blinking rapidly, I willed my mouth to move. "What are the limitations?"

I figured I'd might as well run with the interesting hallucination concept and learn what I could from Joshua's...*ghost?* Was that what was happening? I pressed my lips together, annoyed.

I didn't believe in that stuff. Maybe I'd hit my head and the combination of the annoying Viv and her psychic nonsense, along with discussing the ghost investigator murder with Ana, had somehow caused my brain to concoct this scenario.

"Are you sure you shouldn't seek the help of a physician?"

He smiled, and I found myself wishing Joshua was real. As in really, real, spend some quality alone time with real. I gave myself a mental slap.

No.

No men. My new beginning was all about *me* and what *I* wanted. Wasn't that what I'd told Ana? Besides, hot Joshua was definitely younger than me. Sort of. I guess it depended on how you looked at it. At any rate, he wasn't solid, couldn't touch me and I couldn't touch him. I sighed as I pushed myself up from the floor.

Problem solved.

"I'm fine." I didn't share that my limbs still felt like Jell-O after the shock my system had incurred. "Just let me sit down for a sec." I plopped onto the overstuffed chair. "Then I'd love it if you could explain what the heck is going on."

He nodded, sitting on the sofa next to the chair. I narrowed my eyes as I watched him lower himself onto the cushion, wondering if he could feel the piece of furniture, or if the action was more about behaving in a familiar manner from when he was alive.

I shuddered. *Dead man sitting.*

"I'll do my best, Cate."

My hand shot up, palm out. "Hold on. No offense, but I'm seriously getting tired of people I've never met or spoken to before knowing my name. What gives?"

"I apologize. When you were here with Sylvia, when I tried to get your attention with the jewelry box? I heard her use your name. I remember you from other times, too." He shrugged. "I don't know how long ago that was, time doesn't pass the same for me as it does for the living. It feels as if it were yesterday, but I know it wasn't."

Joshua's shoulders slumped. "I sensed when she passed. It pains me, because I never had the chance to say goodbye. Somehow, I thought I'd see her on this side, but..." He shook his head. "I'm afraid I'm not completely clear how everything works on the etheric plane."

I swallowed down my emotion at his mention of Aunt Sylvia. "Oh. I see." I brushed back a stray curl that hadn't quite made it into my ponytail. "But why were you trying to get my attention? I've been here countless of times, practically grew up in this cabin as much as I visited." I narrowed my eyes at him again. "Wait a minute. Have you been watching me while I, you know, get dressed or at any other extremely inappropriate times?"

He straightened, slapping a palm to his chest. "Of course not. I'll have you know, I'm a gentleman. I hated being treated as if I were nothing but a scoundrel because of my trade as a logger. When I left my family home in Ohio, it was only to make my fortune here in the West." He averted his gaze. "Sadly, the opportunities I sought didn't materialize the way I'd hoped." Joshua locked eyes with me again. "But that's long ago, no longer of any importance."

I cringed. "I'm sorry things didn't go the way you wanted them to." Regardless of anything else, this man's physical life was over, and for whatever reason, he was stuck in between the living and wherever our souls went when we died. "But again, I don't understand why you wanted to get my attention. Why then and not earlier?"

"I imagine you'll think me quite mad, but I was compelled to. It was as if I couldn't help myself." He gestured with his hand, slicing it through the air. "As I said, I can't grasp something in your plane, couldn't help you up. But with enough mental or emotional intent, I've found I'm able to create a burst of energy that is sometimes strong enough to move objects. If nothing else, make a discernible sound."

"Seriously?" I considered his statement. It certainly seemed to match up with all the traditional tales of hauntings, objects moving, creaking floors and so on. "Wait. Are you haunting this cabin?"

Joshua chuckled. "I suppose? Believe me, I wish I knew."

I was becoming frustrated on his behalf. "So, there hasn't been anyone, not even a fellow spirit, *no* one to give you an idea of why you're still here, or what the ghost rules are?"

"For the most part, no." Joshua shook his head. "That's part of the reason I've been so desperate to find someone of your ability who can give me some insight. Sylvia was very clear that the pendant wasn't for her, that it was for someone else. I never understood what she meant, but the last time you were here, I knew. You had the glow."

I arched my eyebrows. "Hold up. That's a lot to unpack right there. I'll get back to the rest of your statement in a bit, but fill me in on what exactly you mean about my ability." I chuckled. "Plus, I wasn't aware I glowed."

Joshua straightened as if I'd said the strangest thing ever. "You have the pendant, correct?"

"Well...yes. So you're saying it's the pendant that makes me glow?" I snorted. "I'm so confused. What is it about me that makes you believe I'm what you've been waiting for?"

"The only people who can see or interact with me are psychics or mediums. Up until the last time you were with your aunt, Sylvia was the only medium I met after I died, but she didn't have the glow. Then I saw you, and I knew my wait was finally over." He flashed his pearly whites again. "I had to make contact, otherwise I wouldn't have knocked over the jewelry box for you to find the pendant." Joshua's shoulders slumped. "I hadn't counted on Sylvia taking it from you."

How could I get this ghost to realize that I wasn't the medium he was looking for? I wasn't psychic, clairvoyant, telepathic or even vaguely sensitive. I rubbed the back of my neck. Although, I *was* sitting in my supposedly psychic aunt's cabin chatting with a dearly departed spirit, so there was that...

"All right, let's try and figure this out." I rose from the chair and began pacing. I held up a finger. "You're convinced Sylvia was a medium—"

"I'm not merely convinced of that fact. I know."

"Okay, sure." I wasn't in the mood to argue with the dead. "And even though I've never shown any predilection toward anything in the supernatural realm and don't even believe...er...didn't believe in such things until about ten minutes ago—I supposedly possess these same skills.

I sucked in a deep breath and bit back the urge to snort before continuing. "In addition, you're unsure why you're still on the earthly plane, and no one from the realm you occupy has bothered to clue you in. Correct?"

He nodded. "For the most part."

I crossed my arms. "Which part am I missing?"

"The part where you don't believe you're psychic and the fact that I haven't had any interaction with other spirits on this side."

I chose to ignore Joshua's insistence that I was psychic for the moment. "Then what the heck *do* you know for sure?"

"That I was killed before my fated time, robbed of the life I was meant to live." He glanced away, and I imagined that this rugged man from another era had been struck with emotion he undoubtedly didn't want a woman to see. Joshua cleared his throat before regarding me again. "That information was given to me by a being who described himself as an angel. I only saw him one other time. That was after Sylvia first saw me, and the angel Camiel, warned me not to become too attached to her, that she wasn't the one."

My eyebrows shot up. "The one what?"

"The medium who would guide me to a deeper understanding of my fate."

I choke-snorted. "Uh...I hope you don't get too attached to me, either." The idea that me, of all people, would be part of some cosmic plan was so ridiculous, I couldn't hold in my laughter. "Sorry, buddy. But you've struck out again."

The laughter died in my throat at the anger blazing from Joshua's eyes. He shot to his feet.

"I refuse to be mocked by someone who thinks they know more than I do regarding the afterlife."

My jaw dropped. "I wasn't mocking you, and I certainly don't think I'm knowledgeable about the afterlife. Especially since I don't—"

"Don't believe in *anything*." Joshua threw his hands in the air.

"So, you've said. If you're so certain I'm not real and that you're not connected to that necklace, then you must have lost your senses, correct? Or perhaps your aunt was also mad as a hatter? Why else would she have been so intent on hiding the pendant from you? Perhaps your entire family is completely insane, in which case, I have no desire to interact with you any longer." He made an exaggerated bow. "Good day to you, madam. I wish you luck in your dreary, unbelieving existence."

I gasped, ready to fire off my own angry retort when Joshua evaporated, his image disappearing as if he'd never been there. No soft, ghostly fade, or wispy tendrils or him floating away, just *poof*. Gone.

My face filled with heat, and I stayed rooted to the spot, clenching my fists in exasperation. Even the ghost haunting my new home thought I was boring. But stronger than my anger was the sickening feeling in the pit of my stomach. The sensation was similar to how it felt to make a horrible mistake, to be dreading the consequences of my actions.

"Dammit."

I had no idea what to do to banish the uneasiness clawing at my insides, but there had to be some sort of solution to this dilemma. However, because I was completely clueless when it came to ghostly pursuits, I knew I'd need help figuring out what to do. Finally able to force my lead feet into motion, I reached for my cell and clicked on the search engine.

Ten a.m. to six p.m. daily. Perfect.

I had an annoying shop owner to visit in the morning.

CHAPTER
FIVE

The tinkling of chimes greeted me as I pushed open the door to Guinevere's Garden. Returning to the shop wasn't something I'd planned on doing so soon, or more accurately, ever. However, I wasn't about to fess up to anyone in my inner circle that a smokin' hot ghost was hanging out at my cabin.

Viv wasn't inner circle. As a matter of fact, she was as outer circle as I could get.

"Well, well, well..." Viv glanced up from where she'd been hunched over the display case, then leaned against the back counter, crossing her arms with a smirk. "Look what the fates dragged in."

"Uh, yeah." I marched toward her with purpose. "I'm not even going to pretend to know what that means." Once I reached the glass case, I slapped down two twenties. "It's forty bucks for a reading, right? Let's do this thing."

She tsked, shaking her head. "What am I going to do with you, Cate?" Viv waved her hand dismissively at the money. "Do you honestly believe this piddling amount of cash is going to offer you clarity in your predicament? Give you the inner knowledge and understanding of what's required of your true self?"

I dug around in my purse for my wallet. "How much then? I've got two credit cards that haven't been maxed out yet."

Viv rolled her eyes then slid the two bills back at me. "Cut the dramatics." She jerked her head toward the room shielded by a dark purple velvet curtain, the very one she and my daughter had disappeared behind the other day. "Let's have a chat." Without waiting for my response, she started making her way to the back, calling out over her shoulder, "You're in charge, Ellwyn. This might take a minute."

Only then did I realize we weren't alone. I'd made a point of arriving at the store the second it opened. I'd been going for anonymity, not wanting to begin my new life with the Squirrel Cove residents thinking I was one of these goofy new age people.

"Ahem."

My head snapped around at the sound of Viv's voice and I saw that she was jerking her thumb over her shoulder.

"Oh, sorry."

After giving the gum-smacking, teenage girl at the other side of the store a self-conscious smile, I scurried away, following Viv into the mysterious unknown. Maybe she was right. Maybe I *was* being dramatic. Then I remembered the lumberjack from 1879 who'd materialized in my living room before vanishing into thin air.

Nah. Not too dramatic.

I squinted as my eyes adjusted to the dim surroundings. Why did everything mystical need to be so dark? I resisted the urge to assume it was because it made it easier to fool people that way. After all, the only reason I was consulting with Viv at all was my begrudging acceptance that ghosts, psychics and who knew what else was my new reality.

Once I was able to see clearer, I noted the small, round table in the center of the approximately ten by ten room, which also seemed to double as storage for backstock. Viv lit a long stick of incense, then placed it in the mouth of a carved green face at the end of an incense holder, the likeness resembling a man with tree branches for hair. She then lit several pillar candles of varying colors, the glow of the flames adding to the minimal light being cast by an ancient-looking stained-glass lamp.

Was I going to have to learn all this magical mumbo-jumbo to survive from now on?

Viv gestured to one of the two folding chairs surrounding the table covered with a velvet cloth similar to the curtain guarding the doorway.

"Have a seat, Cate. And quit looking as if you're about to be tortured." She shook her head with a chuckle. "Being psychic isn't as hellacious as you're making it out to be."

I slid back one of the rickety metal chairs then sat down. I had to hand it to her. She hadn't gone for the ornate carved throne, menacing gargoyle statues or enormous crystal ball atop a jeweled stand. The stacks of cardboard boxes stamped Made in China and the cheap, beat-up furniture didn't exactly scream sideshow attraction.

After wiggling around to get comfortable on the hard surface, I folded my hands on the table and cleared my throat. "So, how does this work? Do you do the palm thing? Tea leaves?"

Viv leaned back in her own chair then propped her feet up on one of the boxes, crossing them at her ankles. "Cut me a break. I do have divination cards of my own design along with other talismans and such. That's what *I* work with when necessary." One corner of her mouth quirked into a smile. "I save the tarot cards and crystals for the tourists."

My eyebrows shot up. *I knew it.* "Then you freely admit you're a hoax."

Viv snorted. "Hardly. But the majority of humanity isn't mentally equipped to handle what I have to offer."

"Wow. I didn't know you were this humble."

Viv yawned, patting her mouth with the palm of her hand. "Can we get past the sarcasm and discuss why you're here? I have a shipment of plastic dragons to price."

The urge to march out and forget this whole business gnawed at me. "Fine. But tell me one thing before we continue. Did you rip off my daughter with a fake reading?"

Viv pinched the bridge of her nose then locked eyes with me. "Look. I know I can get testy. Believe me, when you've been around as long as I have, your tolerance for pretty much everything is nil. However, let me ease your mind. I gave Hailey exactly what she needed to hear, and a helluva lot more than most." Viv jabbed a finger at me. "She's your daughter. I respect that."

I had to admit I was confused. Viv came across as sincere and this was the first time she hadn't been flippant with me. Maybe there was more to the woman than I gave her credit for.

"Thanks." I shifted on the chair, adjusting my sore behind against the unforgiving metal seat. "I appreciate that. But I don't get it. If you have so much to offer—as you put it—then why not go all out? You could make scads of money."

Viv let out an aggravated sigh. "Someday, hopefully soon, you'll discover there's so much more to life than cash—even when there's scads of it." She arched her eyebrows. "Shall we get started? That junk isn't going to price itself."

I was back to being irritated and crossed my arms. "Even though money's not important?"

Viv slid her feet off the box then stretched her arms above her head. "A girl's gotta make a living. Back to more significant matters. Did you bring the pendant with you?"

I almost coughed. "Wha...?" I leaned forward as if spies were listening to us. "What makes you think it's so special? I never showed it to you when I was here."

"Its power called to me the moment you entered the shop. I

knew it was still here on the mountain, but I haven't felt the energy of that necklace in over forty years."

Right as I was about to ask what power the pendant supposedly possessed, something else jumped to the forefront of my mind.

"Wait a second. Forty years?" I chuckled. "That can't be right. You wouldn't have even been born yet."

"Why, thank you." Viv brushed back her curls and batted her eyelashes. "Let's forget about me for now, though, shall we?"

I pressed my lips together. "Fine." I poked my finger at her. "But I want to revisit this subject. Since you claim you're sharing stuff with me that you don't with the tourists, then I want to be filled in on your story."

"Yeah, yeah, yeah. So pushy." Viv folded her hands on the table. "Let's get back to the pendant. I sense you're related to Sylvia, but I'm not picking up in what way."

My throat closed up, and I had to take a deep breath to continue. "She was my great aunt. I recently moved into her cabin and found it when I was going through her things."

Viv nodded sagely as if that explained everything. It explained nothing to me.

"But that's not the whole reason why you're here, is it?"

I narrowed my eyes. "You tell me."

She narrowed hers back. "Don't play games. That pendant holds much power and meaning. It bonds to the one who's meant to wear it. When Sylvia came to me originally, she knew it wasn't meant for her and sought my counsel. It was then that I advised her to tell Joshua it wasn't time, that the one who was meant to give him the answers *he* sought hadn't arrived yet."

After picking my jaw up off the floor, I sputtered, "H-how could you *possibly* know about Joshua?" Once again, dizziness washed over me. "This is insane."

Viv patted the back of my hand. "Calm down. I'm sure I already know the answer to this question, but you have no clue that you're psychic, correct?"

I yanked my hand away, slapping my palms to my face. What the hell was going on? Why was this happening to me? The whole reason I'd moved to Sylvia's charming cabin in the sleepy town of Squirrel Cove was to get some peace and quiet, to relax and take the time I needed to figure out the next phase of my life. Not start up the next Psychic Friends hotline.

"Cate, look at me. I can help you get through this. I know I'm a smart-ass, but seriously. Humans can be so annoying."

I didn't take the bait. She said we could discuss her history later and I wasn't ready for anymore grand supernatural revelations. The magic of the pendant and my so-called psychic powers were enough for one day.

"Yes." My voice wobbled, so I took another breath to steady myself. "I have the pendant with me."

Viv nodded. "Good. For starters, you should be wearing it all the time. That'll go a long way in helping you understand your power. It'll also shield you from those who wish to possess it and misuse its magic. Remember that film with the sparkly red shoes and the mangy dog?" She snapped her fingers as if trying to bring the Wizard of Oz to mind. "Don't let anyone talk you into taking it off. That water trick on witches is an old wives tale." Viv shook her head. "Doesn't work at *all*."

"Good to know." I rubbed my forehead. Why hadn't I thought to keep some Tylenol in my purse? "Beyond not taking off the pendant, what about this psychic stuff. Wouldn't I have noticed by now that I can see the future, or whatever it is fortune tellers are supposed to do."

"Cate, seriously." She shook her head as if I were a child. "You've got to let go of all this stereotypical crap you've been programmed with. You're only making this tougher on yourself."

I growled in aggravation and balled my fists. "Then just *tell* me

58

what's going on. How can I do whatever it is I'm supposed to do if I have no idea what it is I'm doing!"

Viv jerked back her head, eyebrows raised as if I'd smacked her across the face. "Whoa, chill. Rome wasn't built in a day." She snorted. "Trust me, I know. Never thought the damn thing was going to get finished."

"Oh my God," I muttered. As soon as I left Viv's shop, I was heading straight to the liquor store. "Help me out, Viv. I'm not sure how much more my feeble human brain can handle."

She sighed. "Fair enough. Let's start with the basics. You were meant for a certain type of psychic awareness." Viv shook her finger at me. "Not all mystical seers are alike. In your case, the pendant is your destiny, and your powers weren't awakened until you found, and bonded, to it. That's what will keep you going through all the struggles and challenges that await you."

"Yippee. I was wondering when I'd have the joy of experiencing more struggles and challenges."

Viv continued. "Your fate and Joshua's fate are intertwined. Only through working together can you see your way through all you'll be tasked to do."

"And why, pray tell, are we intertwined?"

Viv shrugged. "Haven't a clue. While I can sense the power of the pendant, and am well-versed in medallions of this type, the exact purpose of each one is hidden from me. That knowledge is reserved for the ones who are fated to possess and use it."

I flopped back against the chair in defeat. "Perfect. I'm a clueless psychic. How pointless is that?"

Viv tapped her fingers on the table in seeming annoyance. "It's not pointless. Every journey has a beginning, and this is yours. Embrace it, learn as you go. Be open to new understanding and revelations." She leaned forward, holding my gaze. "And for eternity's sake, go kiss and make up with Joshua. Poor kid has been waiting for decades for the right one to appear." Viv checked her watch. "Ooh, we're going to have to end this. I've got a reading in five minutes."

"Seriously?" I huffed. "I've got a million more questions. I'm completely lost, I'm..." My bottom lip trembled. "I can't do this alone."

"You won't be alone." Viv grinned. "You've got your ghost side-kick. And you can drop in anytime to ask whatever you want." She rose, signaling that the time had come for me to get the heck out of her shop. "Just be forewarned that I'm not able to answer all of them. Rome wasn't built—"

"In a day. Got it." I heaved out a sigh and rose as well. "Be prepared to see a lot of me, though." As I followed her out of the stockroom, another thought occurred to me. "Oh hey. Should I get a deck of cards or be burning certain candles or anything like that?"

Viv glanced over her shoulder with a grin. "I thought you didn't believe in that nonsense?"

"Uh, well... I'm trying, you know, to get onboard or whatever."

Viv barked out a laugh. "I'm yanking your chain. Start with the pendant." She waggled her eyebrows. "That'll keep you plenty busy for a while."

My shoulders dropped, but I nodded in response. She was right. A fated pendant and making up with the pissed off ghost haunting my cabin was enough of an assignment for now.

"Gotcha. But I'll be back."

Viv grinned with a mischievous glint in her eye. "Oh, I'm sure you will."

CHAPTER

SIX

O nce I picked up a bottle of wine—my new breakfast of champions—I headed back to the cabin, anxious to set things right with Joshua. However, I didn't plan on doing any kissing while making up. Not only because I wasn't interested, but it was physically impossible.

As I unlocked my door a wave of melancholy passed over me. Had Joshua left behind a wife and family? I assumed he was the age he appeared to be as a ghost when he died. Then again, our initial meeting had ended before I'd learned that much about the man.

I entered the cabin, placing the bag with my wine that may or may not have also contained a package of cookies on the table with the hurricane lamp. I then steeled myself to face the unknown. Taking a deep breath, I lowered myself onto the chair, angling myself toward the sofa Joshua had occupied the night before. How was I supposed to get him to reappear?

I groaned. I should've at least made Viv tell me that much before leaving. Although, I doubted anyone could make Viv do anything she didn't want to do. Whatever she was supposed to be,

I couldn't deny I was as interested in knowing her story as much as I was Joshua's.

As I contemplated how to proceed, it occurred to me that everything about my situation revolved around the pendant. Viv had been clear I should put it on and never take it off. I jumped to my feet then quickly retrieved my purse. A sense of urgency filled me, as if something dark and foreboding was on the horizon, ready to snatch the necklace from my possession at any second.

I dug through my purse, my shaking fingers closing around the now familiar pouch. Tugging it free, I then quickly undid the ties, retrieving the gold object and letting it rest in my palm. The pendant shone and I gazed at it through new eyes. What mysteries did it hold? And more importantly, what did it all mean for me and Joshua?

I cleared my throat as I held the pendant up by the chain, staring at it intently, shoving aside the disconcerting thought of mine and Joshua's fates being tied to this mysterious piece of jewelry.

"Here goes nothing." I grunted. "Or hopefully, something."

I closed my eyes as I slipped the chain around my neck, and once again, fastened the clasp. This time, I planned to keep it on for good—or at least until I was sure of what was going on.

Heading to the bathroom so I could view it in the mirror, I half expected lightning bolts or a tornado of wind or some other bizarre occurrence to take place. When absolutely nothing happened, I realized Viv was right. I did have a tinge of the dramatic in me.

I stared at my reflection, my gaze fixed on the pendant. I ran my fingers over the infinity symbol, much as I'd done that first time. The obvious meaning of infinity was forever, or more accurately, never-ending. I pinched my eyebrows together. Researching all the possible meanings of the symbol would be a great start in my quest to understand what the heck was happening to me.

But for now, I had to figure out how to get Joshua to reappear. I mentally kicked myself again for not pushing Viv on giving me some pro tips on how to make that happen. As I headed back to the living room, I considered what methods I should employ to summon a ghost. A Ouija board came to mind, but Viv had said I didn't need any extra bells and whistles for now.

I took up residence on my chair again, landing with a thud. "Hmm..." I tapped my fingers on the chair arm, truly lost about what to do next.

"Joshua?"

I glanced around the room, wondering if darkness *was* needed for spirits to appear. Even clichés had their roots in truth.

"Uh, Joshua? Are you here? If you are, I'm sorry about last night. And uh..." I shifted in my seat. "Well, I met with someone today, someone who knows about this kind of stuff. Knows about the pendant." I cleared my throat. "And you. She's the one Sylvia went to years ago, and who told her to let you know Sylvia wasn't the one you were meant to get your answers from.

I sucked in a breath, bracing myself to dive off the cliff into the unknown. "Turns out, you really are stuck with me, but that's okay. I've got help now." I let out a shaky chuckle. "As it so happens, you were right. I'm the one the pendant belongs to after all."

A scream was torn from my throat as Joshua abruptly appeared less than five feet from me. I slapped a hand to my chest.

"*Geez.* A warning would be nice."

"I apologize."

Joshua's expression was hard to read. I couldn't discern whether he was merely stoic by nature, or still cranky over our little tiff the night before.

"Have a seat?" I gestured to the couch.

Joshua regarded the piece of furniture as if deciding whether it was acceptable enough for him to sit on, then lowered himself onto the sofa. His expression remained unreadable as he perched on the edge of the cushion, his hands folded and resting on his knees.

"I'm listening."

I held up the pendant. "Look. I'm wearing it now. That's a start, right?"

His brow furrowed. "A start to what?"

Oh boy. I wondered if Viv did ghost and psychic family counseling.

"Don't you know anything about the origin or meaning of the pendant?" I said hopefully. "What about that angel who gave you some info on your situation?"

He sighed. "Well, yes. But not anywhere near enough to my satisfaction. It would make everything so much simpler if they would come out with it instead of being so evasive."

I threw my hands in the air. "I know, right?" I huffed. "I don't get why everything has to be such a big puzzle."

Joshua gave a sharp nod. "Precisely. That's what I've been saying for decades. At least, whenever I've had the chance." He frowned. "Unfortunately, there haven't been enough opportunities to speak to anyone with that kind of knowledge."

I slumped against the chair. "So, here we are. Neither of us with any idea how to proceed."

Joshua tilted his head. "Wouldn't it make sense to go back to this woman who said she could help you?"

I ran my hand across the top of my head, suddenly hyper aware that I probably looked a wreck. "Yes...and no. Her name's Viv, by the way, and she's a psychic as well. Or something. However, her message today consisted of being patient, us working together on this thing, and to drop in if things got too rough." I shrugged. "At least, that's my interpretation of events."

Joshua tugged at this beard. "Another psychic, hmm? Interesting. Well, perhaps I can tell you more details about myself, help you to understand my situation better. That's as good a place to begin as any, I suppose."

I gasped, grabbing the chair arms in excitement. "Of course, that's it! I've been meaning to go to the Stagecoach History Museum for ages. If nothing else, it'll help me get a feel for this area's past, especially the logging industry. And who knows? There might even be information about you."

Joshua let out a grunt. "I doubt that. I was of little importance."

My stomach twisted. I hated hearing him refer to himself as if he were nothing. "Don't say that. Everyone is important in their own way."

Joshua averted his gaze. "That's debatable. But never mind, I think that visiting this history museum is a grand idea." He shook his head with a chuckle. "I assumed Stagecoach would have died off by now, not have its own museum celebrating the dark days of its past."

"Oh? What do you mean by dark days?" This was the kind of stuff that piqued my interest. "Did you live in Stagecoach at some point?"

"Only briefly. I went there once my gold mining prospects fell through." He turned away. "As it so happened, I was..." He cleared his throat then gave me a tight smile. "Well, let's just say there was a need for men to chop down trees up here on the mountain." Joshua flexed, giving me an eyeful of his impressive gun show. "I didn't have experience, but I had strength. They were desperate for as many workers as they could get, so I didn't have a problem getting hired.

He lowered his head, folding his hands once again. "I don't mind hard work, but I was unaccustomed to the crass nature of the men I met in the camp. While I don't consider myself a snob, I do appreciate civilized behavior."

I frowned, tilting my head. "Huh. Now that you mention it, you don't come across at all like a tobacco-spitting, swearing, crotch-grabbing brute."

Joshua's eyes widened. "Madam!" He pursed his lips as if he'd tasted something sour. "Such language from a lady."

"It was merely an observation." I hmphed. "And watch the 'madam' talk."

Technically, I suppose I qualified for the term—prostitution affiliations aside—but it still grated on my nerves. Embracing forty as the new thirty was near impossible with a sexy, technically younger, man referring to me as if I were his grandmother.

He raised his eyebrows. "I apologize if I made a rash assumption. I didn't realize you're a spinster like your aunt."

I gasped. "Listen, buddy." I jabbed a finger at him. "If we're going to hang out, you need to get better acquainted with modern word usage and connotations. I'm Cate. Not Miss, Madam or... spinster." I crossed my arms. "You don't know anything about me."

Joshua let his head fall back as he dragged his fingers through his hair, his muscles rippling beneath his skin, looking all rugged and hunklicious. I frowned, grateful that the only option in our relationship was a platonic one. I might be dedicated to remaining man-free, but that didn't mean I couldn't be tempted. The last five years of my marriage hadn't exactly been plentiful in that department.

With a sigh, he locked eyes with me again. "You're right. We know very little of each other. I imagine compromises will need to be made on both our parts."

"Spinster isn't up for a compromise. Just sayin'."

He gave a quick jerk of his head. "Agreed."

"Okay, let's see." I rubbed my chin, considering what we had to work with so far. "It's too late to head to Stagecoach tonight, of course, but that can be something for me to do first thing in the morning." I shrugged. "Then, if I find out anything of interest, we can go from there."

My idea didn't seem all that mind-blowing regarding our quest, and Joshua's resigned expression radiated his agreement.

"What about your friend, Viv? Shouldn't you try to meet with her again? Perhaps with whatever information you acquire in Stagecoach?"

"We're not exactly friends." My stomach tightened, as if I'd insulted her. It wasn't like we were enemies. "I mean, we don't really know each other, that's all."

Joshua chuckled. "Like us?"

"Well, yes. I suppose." I uncrossed my legs, then crossed them again on the other side. Why did I suddenly feel as though I were a big jerk? "But that doesn't mean it'll stay that way. After all, we're getting to know each other, right?"

He regarded me then nodded slowly. "Yes. I hope that's the case. While I haven't experienced every single day since my death, it's still been an agonizingly long time to go without having someone to talk to."

My eyes burned. I couldn't begin to imagine how horrible that must be.

"I'm sorry you've had to suffer through that." I swallowed hard. "What did you mean about not experiencing every day, though?"

Joshua's brow furrowed, and he paused before answering. "It's difficult to explain without knowing what it's like on this side of existence. But I suppose the best description would be that time passes in large chunks, rather than hour to hour."

"How do you mean?"

"Well, imagine you fall asleep, but only wake up every few years." He tugged on his beard before continuing. "That's not exactly right, because sometimes I'm aware of my surroundings when it seems as if only a couple of days have passed, yet other times it's closer to a decade."

"Wow." I shook my head. "And are you always in this cabin?

Like, do you ever end up in other places you've been throughout your life? Say for instance, where you came from originally?"

I was back to wondering if Joshua had a family he'd left behind.

Joshua let out a mournful sigh. "I'm afraid not. For reasons I can't fathom, I seem destined to remain inside this tiny house."

I held up my hand. "Don't say that. This pendant," I grasped the disc then held that up instead. "This is the key to changing your fate, remember?" I let it go and sucked in a deep breath before continuing. "Sure, we have very little information on what this all means, but don't worry, we'll figure it out together." I snorted. "It's not as if I have a job or anything. I'll be able to dedicate all my time to your cause."

Joshua frowned. "If you have no work, then you must have a husband to care for you, yet I've seen no man in this home."

"There've been men here before." I scratched my head. "On occasion." Vince had rarely joined me on my visits to Sylvia. "Although, not that often. I suppose it could've been easy enough to miss them since you're not aware of every day."

"But you live here all the time now?" He glanced away. "I imagine your husband will be joining you soon now that you've prepared the household."

"Nope. Just me. I'm divorced."

Joshua whipped his head around and I wanted to smack the Mr. Judgey Pants expression off his face. "You abandoned your family?"

I shook my finger at him angrily. "What was I just saying about not making assumptions, huh? It wasn't exactly my idea, so don't get all critical," I huffed. "And anyway, so what if I was the one who divorced him? Once again, you know *nothing* about me or my life."

Joshua scrubbed his face with one hand. "You're right. If only Sylvia would have interacted with me over the decades, perhaps the modern ways wouldn't be such a big adjustment for me."

"I'm sure she had her reasons."

I didn't appreciate anyone—particularly a rude ghost—saying anything negative about Sylvia.

Joshua lowered his head, nodding. "I hope you didn't take offense. I did like Sylvia quite a bit. Based on our limited interaction, she seemed wise and kind." His brow wrinkled. "It's merely my loneliness that caused me to speak out of turn."

I did need to keep reminding myself that Joshua had been dealt a brutal hand. He might not understand my life, but I had the same issue when it came to understanding his death.

"That's all right. I tell you what—let me fill you in on the basics of my circumstances, then maybe you can share some more background on who you were?"

The corners of Joshua's lips curled into a smile. "I'd like that."

I sucked in a deep breath. "Alrighty then. Well, as you now know, I'm divorced. It was finalized recently, and I decided to move up here to get a fresh start."

"Where did you move from?"

"Los Angeles, so definitely an adjustment."

Joshua arched his eyebrows. "Goodness. You're from the big city. Will you be able to handle living in such a wilderness as this?"

I'd already promised myself to give Joshua a break. We were from different worlds in more ways than one.

"I've got this, I assure you."

He regarded me dubiously. "Well, should you need advice, I'm happy to provide it where I can."

"Sure." I gave him a tight smile. "I'll keep that in mind."

"Do you have children?"

"I do, a daughter. And before you ask, she's an adult, so that's why she isn't living with me."

"I wasn't going to ask." Joshua gave a one-shouldered shrug. "I saw a young woman with you here—I can't give a timeline—and I've seen her change, grow older as time wore on. I assumed she must be your child. And since the last time I saw her, she appeared to be an adult..." He smiled. "I assumed she must have left home to start her own family."

"Bite your tongue." I shuddered. "She's only twenty and it hasn't even been a year yet since she began living with her boyfriend."

Joshua stared at me, shifting around on the sofa as if debating how he should respond. I quickly came to the conclusion that he was struggling with his old-fashioned attitudes toward such things while resisting the urge to insult me again.

"I see." He cleared his throat. "Well, you would know best."

I narrowed my eyes. "That's right. I *would*." I unpursed my lips before continuing. "Anything else you care to know about me?"

He gazed at the ceiling while tapping a finger to his lips. "How old are you?"

"*Excuse* me?" I smacked the chair arm with great vehemence. Man, this guy was asking for it. "Don't you think that question's a tad invasive?"

He held up his hands like he didn't see what the big deal was. "I'll happily share my age. Or rather, my age at the time of my death. I was thirty-four."

I winced. Yeah, I'd figured he was young. But now I knew for sure how young when he'd lost his life.

"Oh man, that sucks. Do you remember...?"

I paused, biting my lip. I'd just chided him for asking invasive questions, and I almost blurted something hugely inappropriate.

"What?" He tilted his head. "Ask what you will. I've no reservations, nothing to hide. Unnecessary secrets lose their significance once you're dead."

I cleared my throat. "Excellent observation. In which case..." I took a big breath before continuing. "I'm forty-two. Which I suppose would be considered an old lady in your former world."

Joshua let out a hearty chuckle, and I curled my fingers into a fist. I wasn't violent by nature, but damn. I didn't need a dead guy laughing at my age. There was also the fact that punching a ghost would be a waste of energy.

He shook his head. "I've learned over the decades that it's different now, that life expectancies have improved." The corner of Joshua's mouth quirked into a smile. "And besides, you don't resemble an old lady in the slightest."

Heat filled my cheeks and I shifted in the chair. I decided to forgive him for his momentary display of amusement.

Joshua's brow wrinkled as he considered me. "What was the question you stopped yourself from asking? You have me quite curious."

I turned away. "It's probably too personal." I tucked one side of my hair behind my ears. "Plus, it would bring up an unpleasant subject." With a light laugh, I shook my head. "Never mind."

"Now I *have* to know."

Glancing up, I met his intense gaze. "Seriously. I don't want to be rude. I've already accused you of that, so it would be bad behavior on my part to do that very thing to you."

He frowned. "Oh please. You've never confronted rudeness until you've worked amongst scoundrels in a logger's camp. Don't be so coy."

I straightened in the chair as images flashed through my mind, reminiscent of the old flickers at the dawn of moviemaking. I couldn't discern the origin of the pictures in my head. Were these thoughts my own imagination? Or were my purported psychic powers beginning to surface and these were actual snapshots from Joshua's life?

"All right. You said you were thirty-four at the time of your death. Do you remember, you know..." I cringed. "How you died?"

Joshua straightened on the sofa as well. "Oh. I'm afraid I don't. Haven't thought about it in ages, either. Initially, the answer to that question plagued me, was all I could dwell on." He sighed. "I wasted the rare opportunities when speaking with those on this side by begging to know the cause of my demise." Rubbing the back of his neck, he shrugged. "What does it matter now? The result is the same."

Joshua's reasoning was solid, but the cause of his death nagged at me, nonetheless. After all, that might be the reason he was stuck on this side instead of wherever it was he'd been meant to travel. It also brought up another question.

"But if you can't remember how you died, how do you know you died at thirty-four? Maybe you were older, but that was the time in your life you were the happiest, so you chose to remain in that form?"

Joshua barked out a laugh. "Hardly. If anything, it was the worst. I'd never choose of my own free will to inhabit this..." He gestured to his clothing. "...This garb of my defeat." He waved his hands around the room. "Or to be doomed to reside in my boss' home that I was forced to build."

I was more confused than ever. "Wait. This wasn't your cabin? I have a photo of you in front of it, posing as if it were. I mean, why take a picture...?"

The expression of pain on Joshua's face stopped me mid-breath and made me feel like a true jerk for bringing up such a sore subject.

"A vain and foolish effort to prove to Cordelia that I was doing well in the west, that she should still wait for me instead of marrying my brother."

Ouch. "I see." I twisted my hands in my lap. So far, I was anything but helpful to Joshua. More like an obnoxious reminder of past agonies. "I'll shut up now."

Joshua dropped his head in his hands and my gut clenched, the weight of his sadness washing over me. This psychic medium stuff wasn't something I'd signed up for and I couldn't fathom how I could help Joshua in a meaningful way. The situation was massively unfair to us both.

Viv might've counseled me to be patient, but she should be prepared for an onslaught of visits anyway. I *had* to get more information about Joshua and the pendant.

Joshua raised his head but wouldn't meet my eyes. "My energy is waning. This is all I can handle tonight."

The faint glow around Joshua's body dimmed then the rest of him slowly faded away. I flopped against the back of the chair, grasping the arms. Right away I had more questions, wished I could continue speaking with him. This time, he hadn't abruptly disappeared. Was his manner of appearing and disappearing by choice or circumstance?

However, that wasn't the most important query. Even if Joshua had given up seeking the answers regarding his premature passing, my inner investigator wouldn't rest until I knew what had happened.

Then perhaps Joshua's spirit could rest, too.

CHAPTER
SEVEN

I sipped my second cup of morning coffee as I flipped through the old pictures my aunt had saved. So many questions had swirled through my head all night, so much so that I'd barely slept. In addition, I'd tried—with zero success—to repeat the flickering images that jumped into my mind while talking to Joshua. I thought if I could slow them down, maybe there would be clues to what happened to him in his final days.

But clearly, my so-called powers weren't easily harnessed. Then again, I'd gotten a late start in life. I probably needed more practice, which was undoubtedly Viv's reason for warning me to be patient.

Draining my coffee mug of the last dregs of dark roast, I debated having a third. I set the photos onto the side table and rose from the chair. Yeah, I needed more caffeine for sure. Right as I smacked the side of my old coffeemaker and it gurgled to life, my cellphone rang. I checked the ID and saw it was from Hailey.

"Hey, sweetie. What's up?"

"Hey, Mom. Not much, just checking in."

With a smile, I leaned against the kitchen counter made from a giant slab of pine. "Well, it's great to hear from you."

I had to admit that I hadn't expected her to call. Back when I lived in L.A., it rarely happened. Of course, when she wasn't busy with her own newly adult life, she could merely drop by for a visit.

Not anymore.

"Are you settling in okay up there? I mean, anything new?"

A lot was new, but nothing I could share with her. Nobody was getting *this* secret out of me. Especially since there was still a small chance I was delusional and in need of professional help.

"It's only been a few days." I chuckled as if it was all so boring. "Just relaxing, that's all."

"Did you ever find out anything else about that pendant, or the old pictures? You know, while you were putting things away? It's killing me not knowing what it's all about and why Aunt Sylvia never told you about them."

I let out a shaky laugh. "Oh, you know. All those things are probably not as exciting as we think they are."

Guilt washed over me at the white lie. This wasn't who I was, yet at the same time, did Hailey really need to worry about her mom going batshit crazy all alone in the mountains?

After a pause, Hailey responded, "I don't know about that. I've never seen anything as cool as that pendant before. If nothing else, maybe you should get it appraised. It might be some sort of valuable artifact or something. It definitely seemed like real gold."

"Maybe someday I will." A change of subject was sorely needed. "Oh, I was going to call you this week and let you know I'll be in town Sunday night. Ana invited me to go to the filming of Real Ghostly Encounters. She's working the show again."

"Ooh, I wish I didn't have to work! I'd totally love to go watch them catch ghosts."

I scratched the back of my head, forgetting how much Hailey

was into this sort of thing. "I don't think you'll be missing much. Ana said all they're doing is taping some segments to insert later, so there won't be any actual hunting."

"Because of Stan's death?"

I frowned at my phone. Did I really know so little of what my daughter was into?

"You know about that?"

Hailey snorted. "Well, duh. It's like my favorite show. Dirk is my favorite investigator—he's so hot. But Stan was more, I dunno, scientific? He only ever claimed to be sensitive, but it seemed as if his psychic abilities went beyond that. On the other hand, Dirk always connects with spirits. It's way cool."

"Huh."

Maybe I could up my psychic game by hanging out at that show. My eyes widened. What if I was able to determine whether Stan died by accident or was murdered? I gritted my teeth. What if Stan's ghost showed up and needed my help like Joshua? The last thing I needed was another dead pal looking for answers in the afterlife.

"Mom? Did you hear me?"

I gave myself a mental shake. "Sorry, what were you saying?"

"Just that we should all go out to dinner while you're in town. I'll ask Ian what his schedule is like."

"Oh. Right. That sounds great, sweetie."

I kept forgetting that my daughter had a partner now, someone she lived her life with.

After chatting a few more minutes and her promising to get back to me with the times she'd be free, I ended the call. My mind kept swirling, imagining scenarios where Stan appeared out of nowhere the way Joshua had. What I needed to do was research all I could about his death before going to the set.

Right as I was about to make my way to the small desk at the other end of the room where I kept my laptop, I realized I was being pulled off track. Today was about going to Stagecoach and focusing on Joshua's plight. For whatever reason, our destinies were tied to the mystery pendant I wore, and that had to be my priority. After all, I wasn't Miss Marple, and I needed to quit acting as if I were.

I snorted. *In theory.*

I perched on the wooden chair—that I'm sure my butt would soon demand I replace with an actual office chair—and woke up my laptop. It would probably be wise to verify that the tiny museum was open before I traveled down the mountain.

After perusing their basic website, I noted the limited hours. They were closed on Mondays and only open from noon to four the rest of the time, which wasn't surprising. Stagecoach might be historic, but it was basically a gas and food stop along the interstate for travelers on their way to somewhere more impressive.

Judging from the photos of the battered, clapboard exterior, the two rusty, broken-down wagons on either side of the small building and a life-sized fake horse tied to the wood railing of the front porch—Disneyland had nothing to fear in terms of tourist competition.

I sighed. "Okay, Joshua. Let's hope this isn't just a waste of time."

"Agreed."

With an embarrassing yelp, I jumped in my chair, grabbing my mug before it could fly off the desk and send coffee everywhere.

"Seriously, Joshua." I frowned up at him. "Must you randomly appear out of nowhere when I think I'm alone?"

He crossed his arms. "I apologize. Being able to freely communicate with the living is unusual for me as well."

I groaned, rubbing my forehead. "Okay, work in progress for both of us. Anyway, I'm about to go get ready to head down the mountain. By the time I reach the museum, they should be opening."

After I snapped the lid to my laptop closed, I rose from my chair. Joshua's gaze remained trained on my computer. My aunt had never been interested in the latest technological advances, so television and a cellphone were probably the two most advanced electronics Joshua had been exposed to.

I pointed at my laptop. "I take it you've never seen one of these before?"

Joshua shifted from foot to foot, almost as if he was embarrassed by his lack of knowledge. "I want you to know that I came from an educated family. In fact, the expectation was that I would follow in my father and grandfather's footsteps and be an attorney.

He turned away, strolling to the picture window that looked out onto the front yard that featured an enormous cedar. Another cabin, much larger and built more recently, was barely visible through the patch of forest that separated us.

"But that wasn't the life I envisioned for myself." Joshua crossed his arms, his shoulders held back and his chest out, his form straight and proud. He'd reached his full height, which I knew was at least a couple inches over six feet. "I revel in the outdoors, in using my hands. Not sitting behind a desk all day, smoking cigars and drinking brandy." He turned back to me, arching a lone brow. "Some whiskey or cider, most certainly." Joshua faced the window again. "But not in cut crystal glasses or a stuffy drawing room."

A clearer picture of Joshua's life and who he was as a man began to form. "I take it that Cordelia preferred crystal and polished silver over whiskey and the great outdoors?"

Joshua grunted. "And my brother, wearing a top hat, tails and a handlebar moustache, no doubt." He regarded me with a wry smile. "She was an opera fan. Not much in the way of the finer arts to offer her out here in the wild west, I'm afraid."

"Didn't she understand what a different type of life it would be out here? I mean, I imagine there were many perils making your way across country, and plenty of adversity after you arrived." I shook my head. "What was she expecting?"

Joshua gave a slight shrug. "We heard many stories, of course. Men slaughtered by Indians, disease, horrible living conditions... But there was also the promise of great swaths of land." He regarded me with a wry smile. "Along with the almighty lure of gold. If anything could inspire Cordelia to leave Cleveland, it was the riches that might be had. In her mind, I would make my claim, unearth a princely sum of the precious stuff, then we could build a grand home in either Los Angeles or San Francisco." He dropped his gaze. "But as the years wore on, she grew weary of waiting.

He lifted his eyes. "I don't blame her, really. Why would a fine lady of her upbringing want to hitch her wagon to a man chopping wood and barely getting by? One who was still living in a tent in a filthy camp of equally filthy men?" He let out another mournful sigh. "She'd already been waiting for so long and was nearing the age of twenty-two without being wedded. I know it was an embarrassment for her family considering their social circle."

"Twenty-two, huh?"

"Yes. We were engaged right before I left to make my fortune, when she was eighteen."

I wanted to add some commentary regarding child brides, but kept my mouth shut. Joshua's world was different than mine, and I needed to keep reminding myself of that.

"So, let me see if I have this straight. You were gone four years, meaning you arrived in California when you were thirty?"

"Yes. I tried to make it work in Ohio first, tried to establish a law career. But the west kept calling my name, and I when I heard about the discovery of gold in these mountains... I couldn't resist taking a chance."

I frowned. "Here?" I pointed at my toes as if there were gold nuggets surrounding my feet. "In Squirrel Cove?"

Joshua's jaw ticked. "That was the news from the west, and many left their homes behind to find their fortune. I made haste so I wouldn't miss out."

As a history buff, and having been raised in California, I probably knew more than the average bear about the Gold Rush. And of the many things I was sure of, was the fact that by the 1870s, panning for gold had come and gone in California for the most part, and never had there been a big find in these mountains. Maybe Joshua was mixing up his details. After all, he'd been dead for almost a hundred and fifty years. He couldn't remember *everything* perfectly.

"I don't mean to contradict you, but I've spent a lot of time in these mountains, and I know quite a bit about California history. As far as I know, there's never been any gold up here."

Joshua's shoulders dropped. "You're right. There hasn't. Why do you think I was chopping down trees?"

Oh. "Yikes. You were scammed?"

"Brutally. I gave the man who claimed to have the rights to the entire mountain a hundred dollars for my own spot to work by the river running through Blackberry Meadows. All the money I had in the world. It was the same for many others. He printed remarkably well-done land deeds, showing us proof of his ownership, then enlisted a cohort to deliver us the deeds we'd paid for. Only after we began digging and panning, did we discover we'd been fooled. The logging company that was the true owner of the property threatened to have us arrested."

"Let me guess. As long as you worked for them, they let you off the hook."

Joshua nodded. "And so my fate was determined."

I crossed my arms, angry on Joshua's behalf. "What a lousy trick. Were those two scammers caught at least?"

"They were." Joshua seemed reluctant to continue.

"Well? Was justice served?"

"Western justice was. My former profession as a lawyer was of no use to me here, since transgressions were handled in their own unique way back then. So, with my gold prospects dashed, all I had left was my strength to offer in seeking employment."

"Wow."

I plucked at my jeans and looked away, not sure what else to say. I'd seen enough western movies in my day to know what he meant by western justice. I couldn't banish from my head the picture of a man swinging from a tree by his neck.

Had Joshua suffered the same fate as well? Perhaps such a gruesome end was too traumatic to bear, and he'd locked it away in his mind, refusing to acknowledge to himself the awful truth.

With a deep breath, I rose, brushing my palms on my jeans. The only hope I had in finding out what happened to Joshua was to get busy and start investigating.

"You're leaving now?" Joshua stood, his expression clouded by what I imagined were painful memories.

"Yeah. Like I said, if I get moving, I can be there when the museum opens." I drew my eyebrows together. "It's a bummer you can't come with me. But I'll take lots of notes." I shrugged. "Who knows? Maybe they have a gift shop that sells picture postcards from that era, or perhaps a local historian has put together his own book that has info we could use."

Joshua nodded, but he wouldn't meet my eyes. "This damnable state I'm in, unable to do anything to help myself." He regarded me with a melancholy expression. "Thank you. Despite our rocky beginning, I believe you're meant to be the one who leads me to my destiny." He chuckled with no humor. "Whatever that might be."

I scraped my teeth along my bottom lip. His dark mood tugged at my heart, the long years of his earthly imprisonment a tangible ache in my body, as if it had happened to me.

My eyes widened. Was I experiencing one of the aspects of my new abilities? This longing to be free, to know why, to no longer be afraid and alone. My throat clogged with emotion, and I swiped at my eyes. I refused to collapse into a blubbering mess. The past year for me had been filled with enough of that nonsense.

"Uh, well..." I coughed into my fist. "Better get moving. No time like the present and all that."

Joshua straightened. "Of course. I'll leave you to it."

An awkwardness had materialized between us, and I couldn't figure out why. We gave each other a small nod then he faded away the same as he had before. At least I was becoming more accustomed to the fact that I had a ghost for a roommate.

As I put the finishing touches on my hair, I considered the rollercoaster of emotions that had passed between me and Joshua. Had he also felt my energy, sensed that the connection between us went both ways?

Frowning, I tugged on the hem of my shirt, leaving one button at the top open so only the chain of the pendant was visible. Somehow, blue plaid and ancient golden amulet didn't seem like it would mix all that well.

I dabbed sunscreen on my forehead and cheeks. Was the pendant ancient? I grunted. Who knew? It sure would be nice if Viv would cough up a few details about what was truly going on.

After grabbing my purse and making sure I had a small notebook and pen on hand, I gave one last glance to my surroundings. For some odd reason, it seemed wrong to leave Joshua behind. The trip was all about his life, dedicated to finding clues to why he was stuck haunting my cabin.

With a small shake of my head, I slung my bag over my shoulder then made my way to the car.

It is what it is.

I climbed in then tossed my purse onto the passenger seat. The engine had barely turned over when something flashed in the corner of my eye, and I turned my head to see what it was.

"What the...?"

My jaw went slack. Staring back at me with eyes bugged and mouth agape was Joshua.

EIGHT

"Cate?"

"Joshua?"

I pinched the bridge of my nose. At least we remembered each other's names.

Joshua reached out, placing his hands on the dashboard of the car, rubbing his palms along the surface.

"I-I'm inside a motorcar." Joshua turned to me with a grin. "I'm not in the cabin." He shook his head with a chuckle. "Obviously." He continued running his hands along the interior of the vehicle. "But this is unbelievable, so fantastic."

I couldn't argue with him there. "Can you feel physical objects on this plane?"

Joshua wiggled his fingers, staring at them briefly before regarding me. "Not in the same way I once did." He snorted. "Although, the memory of that sensation continues to dim with time. I would say it's similar to what it's like when I gather energy to move an object. There's resistance, but I can't discern the finer features of a physical item.

He lowered his head. "I miss the feel of brushing my fingertips across the rough bark of a tree, of petting the soft fur of a dog, the biting chill of river water running over my skin."

I sniffed as my eyes burned. *Great.* If he didn't stop soon, I was in danger of becoming s weepy mess. My chest tightened and I sucked in a deep breath with a new resolve. No matter what it took, I'd help Joshua however possible so he could be released from the awful purgatory he'd existed in for so long.

Shaking off my gloom, I rubbed my palms together. "But this is good, right?" I placed my hand over the pendant concealed by my shirt. "It has to be the pendant that's made the difference."

He arched his eyebrows. "Or the fact that you're wearing it. You left the cabin with it to go to the shop, but I couldn't accompany you then."

"Good point." I inclined my head. "Were you *trying* to follow me?"

Joshua chuckled. "I wasn't trying to follow you now. As always, I assumed I was trapped in the cabin the way I've always been. I haven't even been in the yard since my death."

I winced thinking of how tiny the space was that he'd been stuck in for so long.

"Well, other than the fact that I'm wearing the necklace this time, was there anything else that was different?"

He ran a palm across the top of his head. "I suppose I'd have to say it was a wish. I watched you leave from the living room window and wished I could go, too. Next thing I knew, here I was."

"That makes sense."

In truth, it didn't. But at the same time, none of what had happened since I found the pendant did. Making a wish with the expectation it would come true was probably as old as humanity. Why couldn't Joshua's simple yearning be the catalyst that broke the bonds of his ethereal prison?

"You think so?" Joshua appeared hopeful.

"Sure." This poor guy could use some positivity. "I mean, why not? We could always test it out. Why don't you go back inside then try to do it again?"

Joshua shook his head with vehemence. "No. I won't squander this chance to be free from that cabin—even if it's only a brief moment of time. I'd rather you stick with the plan of going to the museum and seeing what happens with that." He sighed. "Maybe I'll be yanked from the car the second you leave the driveway."

"Don't think that way." I was operating in the dark, but the need to help Joshua was becoming more compelling than ever. "Have you noticed how you don't lose energy like you did before, that you're able to manifest for much longer? I think the pendant is making a big difference all the way around. So, let's hope for the best. I'll wish, too."

I screwed my eyes shut, wondering why I hadn't picked up some of those crystals or runes or whatever to help me out. With as much intention as I could, I pictured Joshua by my side, in the car, at the museum...

A quick flash of being with Joshua in an incredibly inappropriate place jumped in my head and I frantically tried to shove it aside.

Housecleaning, bills, taxes, healthy foods, my ex-husband...

Yeah, that was the one. All amorous inclinations were annihilated.

My eyes flew open, and I noted that Joshua was regarding me with one corner of his mouth quirked. "What are you doing?"

I frowned then shoved the key into the ignition.

"Wishing. What do you think?"

His eyes narrowed a bit, and I turned my attention to driving. As I backed out of the driveway then headed to the main highway, I remained tense. Would he be yanked from the car the way he feared? I could sense his tension as well, and figured he was waiting for the inevitable to happen.

The silence between us stretched on, until halfway down the mountain, it seemed as if I could breathe again.

I grinned. "I think it worked."

"I think you're right."

Joshua still had his hands on the dashboard, his fingers curled as if attempting to hang on. I realized that riding in a car, and going so fast, must be a startling experience for him.

I glanced at him before returning my gaze to the road. "What's it like being in a car for the first time?"

He let out a shaky laugh. "Let's just say I'm grateful that certain bodily functions aren't an issue for me in spirit form."

My eyebrows shot up, my imagination going in all directions. "Feel like elaborating?"

"I'm afraid if I were still among the living, I'd be sick from all this winding around at a fast clip."

"Oh."

He huffed. "What did you think I was going to say?"

I tightened my grip on the wheel, heat filling my cheeks. "That was one."

Joshua crossed his arms. "And the other?"

"You know..." I shrugged. "Sometimes when people are scared, they pee their pants."

He gasped. "Madam! I'll have you know that not only am I not *scared*, neither am I in the habit of urinating on myself. I was merely pointing out that such reckless travel isn't something I'm accustomed to."

"Sorry." I shifted in my seat. "But watch the 'madam' talk, remember?"

"Duly noted." Joshua stared straight ahead, his arms still crossed.

I continued my way down the winding mountain road, careful when taking the hairpin turns. Even if Joshua was unable to hurl all over my car, I wasn't trying to make him uncomfortable.

We were back to being silent, and for my part, I kept my mouth shut to allow myself the time to ponder what lay ahead. Stagecoach wasn't exactly a bustling metropolis, so I didn't want to get my hopes up. I might be about to find out a whole lot of nothing.

I glanced sideways at Joshua who seemed deep in concentration. His gaze remained fixed ahead with his eyebrows pinched together and forehead wrinkled. Did he fear what we might discover at the museum? No matter what, I'd be there for him as a friend.

At last, we arrived at our destination. The museum was located at the far end of Stagecoach where the few remaining ramshackle storefronts of the historic downtown area remained. A big box store along with fast food restaurant options anchored the new downtown at the extreme opposite end of the small town. It was as if the shiny, modern businesses didn't want the stain of the past to curse them.

The parking lot next to the hacienda style building allowed for no more than six vehicles. I imagined the need for all the spaces at one time was low. Even though a major Interstate cut through Stagecoach, I doubted it was on any must-see lists.

Once I cut the engine, I turned to Joshua. "Okay, let's give this a shot."

He lifted his eyebrows. "Shot?"

"You know, a try. See if you can follow me into the museum."

Joshua nodded but wouldn't meet my gaze. "Right. Although, perhaps I can wait here."

I blinked several times. "Why would you want to do that? This is your big day out."

Joshua pursed his lips as he regarded me with those breathtaking green eyes. "Is that what this is? A big hurrah? What if it's instead the day I find out something I don't want to know? What if I discover that my name has been sullied and that history has judged me unfairly?"

While I was pondering what questions to ask the museum personnel on the way down the mountain, poor Joshua had been stressing about potential unsavory revelations. I needed to tread carefully. In truth, Joshua could be quite helpful by steering me in the right direction. On the other hand, he could be having second thoughts regarding what I might find.

Sometimes ignorance really was bliss. And as he'd already commented, it wasn't as if finding out what happened to him would change anything. Still, the answer to why he was stuck on this plane and how he could be released from purgatory might be part of discovering the truth.

"Let's think positive." I gave him the sincerest smile I could manage. I'd never been the best of fibbers, but I was willing to give it my all to help encourage Joshua along. "I bet if there's anything in this museum about you, it's wonderful." I shook my fist in a show of enthusiasm. "Maybe we'll find out you were the best tree cutter in the history of lumberjacking."

Joshua's head slowly turned to face me, his expression one of confusion. "Tree cutter? Lumberjacking?"

I fiddled with my keys and cleared my throat. "You know what I mean. Anyway, let's go. I doubt you can tell, but it's getting toasty in this car."

He heaved out a sigh. "Yes, I remember the dreadfully hot days. Even on the mountain there were times I wasn't sure I could survive the heat." He regarded me with a wry smile. "Especially when I was lumberjacking."

I rolled my eyes and opened the door, glancing over my shoulder. "Well? Are you coming?"

After a beat, he suddenly appeared in front of me, and I let out a cry.

"I gotta ask. Was that intentional?" My heart was still pounding double time.

"Again, all I did was intend to come with you. I'm not sure if I can control the manner in which I appear."

I climbed out of the car, only then realizing that he'd been sitting on my purse for the entire ride. I suppose it didn't matter to him, but I wondered if his ghost butt had left an imprint.

"Okay, we'll table that conversation for later." I reached in to grab my purse then straightened again. My bag was imprint free. "Because it sure would be nice not to have a heart attack several times a day."

"I apologize." He did seem sorry.

"Learning curve." I smoothed down my shirt. "All right. Let's do this thing."

"Do this...?" He shook his head. "Lead the way. I'll defer to you."

Since I was the one who was still alive between the two of us, I would've thought that was a given.

"Thanks." I'd kept most of the sarcasm out of my voice.

As I approached the front of the building, the old wagon wheels from a bygone western era were exactly as they'd been pictured on the website. I knocked on the life-size plaster horse and a quarter-sized chunk of his hide fell off.

"Oops."

It seemed as if Trigger had seen better days. I rubbed the back of my neck, hoping I wouldn't have to cough up some serious dough to pay for the damage.

"You shouldn't touch things that don't belong to you."

I whipped my head around to scowl at Joshua. "It was an accident. I was checking to see what he was made of."

Joshua leaned in to examine the faded, cracking, busted up horse. "Not of very good quality." He straightened. "More reasons not to touch."

I rolled my eyes. "Yes, Daddy."

No sooner had the words sailed past my lips did I start choking on my own spit. What the hell was wrong with me? I could only hope the non-parental meaning was lost on someone who hailed from the nineteenth century.

He frowned. "Why, in heaven's name, are you referring to me as your father?"

Phew. For once, historic differences were working in my favor.

"Never mind." I coughed into my fist. "But we should head inside."

It was unlikely that a huge rush to visit the museum was about to occur, but a diversion was definitely in order. Besides, if I didn't glean anything of interest from the museum, then I might head to the library to do some more research.

As I pushed open the old wooden door that appeared as if a minimum of forty-seven layers of paint had been slapped on the surface over the years, it released a groan of epic proportions. No sneaking into this joint.

"Goodness!" Joshua blurted. "The owners of this establishment clearly have no regard for maintenance. Does no one of this era have any pride in their craftsmanship?"

"Excuse me?" I huffed. "Are you smack-talking my cabin? Aunt Sylvia was very old when she passed, and it wasn't her fault she couldn't keep up with the maintenance. She did the best she could."

The loud clearing of a throat behind me made me jump. I tried to compose myself before turning around to face the person who likely thought I'd lost it. Not that I still wasn't sure that was the case.

"Hey..." I chuckled shakily. "You're open, right?"

The grizzled old man narrowed his eyes at me. "We are." He gazed past my shoulder toward the door that had finally managed to crawl its way shut. "Is there someone else in your party?"

"My...?" I let out a light laugh. "Oh, no. It's just me." I waved my hand around casually. "You're probably wondering who I was talking to."

I licked my lips, frantically searching for a reasonable explanation. I had nothing.

Joshua whispered, "Tell him you're feeling faint from the heat."

I snorted. "It's not *that* hot."

"Ma'am, I'm not sure I understand what you're talking about," said the old man, his head tilting as his eyebrows dipped lower. "Are you all right?"

I had so many answers to that question, but I needed to focus on the actual reason for my visit.

"Oh, I'm fine. Just having a rough week. Uh, by the way..." I hooked a thumb over my shoulder. "I accidentally knocked some of the plaster off your horse outside." I winced. "Sorry. I'd like to pay you for the damage."

The old man grabbed his belly and let out a croaking laugh. "The only thing you can pay me for is for someone to haul away that eyesore. I've been trying to talk the city into doing that for years. They say it gives the place character." He leaned in conspiratorially, covering his mouth with one hand as if the place was bugged. "I say they've been smoking too much wacky tobaccy, if you catch my drift."

My eyebrows shot up. "Oh, uh, yeah. Drift definitely caught."

He was back to narrowing his eyes at me. "Are you here to use the restroom, or to visit the museum? Either way, it's five bucks." He shot out his hand, palm up.

"Museum."

I dug around in my purse and found a loose bill that was folded in half. After retrieving it, I discovered it was a ten-dollar bill. I offered it to him.

"I ain't got no change."

Of course he didn't. "That's all right. Consider it a donation." I gave him a tight smile.

"Why, thank you, ma'am." He broke into a grin. "Help yourself to a complimentary postcard."

I tracked the direction where he was pointing and noted a mostly empty postcard carousel perched on a small glass display case. Upon investigation, I saw that there was only one design available.

The plaster horse out front.

I plucked the bent card from the carousel then turned it over. Squinting, I read the tiny description on the back.

"Bandero, horse belonging to the notorious Lance Johnson, scammer of over fifty would-be gold miners."

"That's him!" Joshua cried out.

Whipping my head around to face Joshua, I pointed at the postcard. "You mean this guy?"

"I'm over here, ma'am," said my grizzled host.

Joshua made a shooing motion, and I gave myself a mental slap before turning to the old man.

"Sorry. Got confused there for a sec. Uh, what can you tell me about Lance Johnson, the man who owned this horse?" I chuckled. "The real horse, I mean."

The man scratched his chin through a scraggly arrangement of silver chin hairs. "Oh, that's one of our most notorious tales. Back in the 1870s, this here Lance and a buddy of his cooked up a grand scheme. They managed to convince a bunch of desperate, not-so-bright fellows that there were gold nuggets in the Blackberry Meadows River." He shook his head. "Probably the news of post-gold rush panning opportunities down in San Diego around that time gave them the idea."

"That's true." Joshua interjected, whispering as if the old man could hear him. "The stories were in the paper, and someone from down south said he'd seen a small bag of nuggets for himself. A prospector was turning them in at a bank down there."

I returned my attention to the old man. "Wow, that *is* quite a tale." I shifted on my feet, racking my brain to come up with a reason to mention Joshua. "What about the people he and his partner scammed? What happened to them?"

The old guy scratched his belly then the top of his head. Apparently, he was a very itchy man.

"Not sure about all of them, of course. But several took jobs with the lumber company on the mountain. Some drank themselves to death." He shook his head sagely. "Terrible thing having your dreams dashed like that. A lot of folks settled in Stagecoach because they had no choice. All their assets were poured into making it out here in the west. Whether it was gold, silver or other promises of riches, they took their chances. Didn't work out for most."

I stole a sideways glance to check in on Joshua, but he wasn't there. I bit my lip, worried that this visit had been a bad idea. Maybe stirring up old hurts had done more harm than good. But there *had* to be a way to find out more.

"Do you have an area of the museum that covers the history of the loggers on the mountain?"

"Sure do." He gestured to a doorway on the other side of the entrance. "That room there is dedicated to the people who settled on the mountain."

"Thanks." I smiled. "I recently moved to Squirrel Cove, so I thought it would be nice to learn more about my new home."

"Well, whaddya know." He grinned. "Welcome to the area. I'm Chester, by the way. Chester Donohue."

He held out his hand and I accepted it in mine.

"I'm Cate McAllister. Nice to—"

My breath caught in my throat as a charcoal gray, shadowy figure appeared next to Chester. I shuddered at the sight of the undulating, featureless mass and a chill ran up my spine.

"Cate! Let him go!" Joshua yelled, his voice muffled as though he were speaking through a pillow.

My ears rang, my stomach churning. I couldn't move. Finally, I sucked in a massive gulp of air, the sensation of my arm being harshly yanked back startling me out of my daze.

"Ma'am? Are you sure you're okay?" Chester regarded me with concern. "I hope you don't take offense, but you've been acting awful strange ever since you got here."

I scanned the immediate vicinity surrounding him, but the creepy image was gone. Then I checked the rest of the room, noting that Joshua wasn't there, either. Where was he when I heard him call out my name?

I let out a long exhale. "It's been a strange week. But thanks. I'm totally fine." I brushed my sweaty palms along my jeans. "I think I'll go check out that room."

"All righty then. Just let me know if you have any questions."

After thanking Chester for his help, I scurried to the area he'd directed me to. My adrenaline remained high from the shock of seeing the dark figure next to Chester, but I needed to concentrate. Then, I needed to go home and crack open a bottle of wine.

"That's him." Joshua abruptly materialized next to me, pointing at a large photograph of a field littered with felled trees. "That's the bastard who was my boss."

This psychic nonsense was seriously getting on my last good nerve. Maybe Viv had some spell or something to reverse the whole thing.

"Joshua? What did I say about appearing out of nowhere?" I placed my hands defiantly on my hips in the same 'I'm not kidding' stance I'd always used with Hailey. "I know we're still figuring all this out, but that would be a truly awesome place to start."

Joshua crossed his arms, adopting a similar stance as he angled his body to me. "I see. And I suppose you'll start berating me for calling you madam, too. Why is that Chester fellow allowed to refer to you that way, but it's a horrible offense if I do?"

95

Oh boy. "Seriously?" I shuddered, the memory of the fore-boding shadow figure still scratching at my brain. "I didn't like it any better when he did it. But I introduced myself and now he knows my name." I stiffened. "Wait. That *was* you, wasn't it? Yelling for me to let him go, I wasn't imagining that?"

"That was me." His lips were set in a hard line. "You must never do that again."

"Shake someone's hand?"

He shook his head vehemently. "Not if their time is near."

"Their time?" I was almost afraid to ask. "You mean...?"

Joshua peered over his shoulder as if Chester might hear him. "One of the few things I learned from the angel who visited me, is that as people near their time to leave the earthly plane, a shadow figure marks them for death."

I shuddered again, my entire body vibrating. "Then what?"

"Then, when Death is ready to take another soul, he searches for the ones with shadow figures attached."

I frowned. "Just anyone? Like, if our buddy Death is hanging out at the gym and there's someone with a shadow figure attached, he just grabs them because they're the most convenient?"

Joshua's brow furrowed. "Sort of? The sense I got was that sometimes it can be overwhelming for Death, so he needs help to stay on track."

"Poor baby." I almost rolled my eyes, then thought better of it. I didn't want Chester's shadow figure to get any cute ideas. I cringed. "Wait. So, it's the shadow figure and not Death that decides who goes?"

"Not at all. It's Death's calling. But you have to admit that it's a huge responsibility."

Discussing the role of Death was beginning to bum me out, but I had to know one more thing. "And you still don't remember how you...?"

Joshua shook his head and shrugged. "Again, no recollections at all, either right before or right after."

As it turned out, I had to know one *more* thing. "What about Chester? Is he...?" I peered past Joshua, checking to see if Chester was near the door getting quite the earful of crazy Cate talking to herself again. "Is he sick or something?" I couldn't quite bring myself to use the D word.

"I have no idea, sorry. But I recognized what was attached to him, and I feared it would mark you because of your powers."

"If I had true powers, I'd fight it off." I huffed. "Somehow, the fact that I'm more susceptible to death and danger because I have these powers doesn't do much to get me excited about cultivating them."

I regarded the exhibit again. "What else can you tell me about your boss other than the bastard part?"

"His name was Sherman. Sherman Miller. The Miller family owned a massive Texas cattle ranch. Sherman Sr. had already built one fortune through ranching and saw an opportunity to expand his riches by sending his son out west. My boss was a spoiled, ne'er do well who reveled in the misfortune of others. A part of me feels he was in on the gold scheme all along, that he'd discovered the perfect way to press men into labor. We'd be forced to stay on no matter how awful the working conditions were, so that we wouldn't be prosecuted.".

"Hmm. That rings true." I stared down at the image of the sour-faced man. "What a jerk." I looked up at Joshua. "Do you think he killed you?"

Joshua abruptly straightened, appearing startled. "Is that what you think? That someone killed me? I might simply have fallen ill, you know. The living conditions were horrible."

"True. I didn't mean to upset you by suggesting foul play. But you have to admit, thirty-four is awfully young to die if you were in generally good health." I pinched my eyebrows together. "Were you in good health?"

"Fit as a fiddle." He puffed out his chest. "But we still don't know for sure if I was the age I appear to be now at the time I died."

I rubbed my chin. "Right..." Joshua and I seemed to be on the same wavelength when it came to many things. Perhaps there was something to all this fated nonsense after all. "Okay, let's see what else we can find while we're here." I waved my hand around. "If any of this stuff rings a bell, let me know."

Joshua heaved a sigh. "I must confess that many of these photos bring back unpleasant memories—even those having nothing to do with me." He gave me a soft smile. "But I do appreciate all you're trying to do, Cate. Please don't think otherwise."

I quickly glanced away. No one should be that handsome when they smiled. "No problem. Hopefully, we won't be wasting our time here today."

Joshua let out another mournful sigh. "I'm afraid that wasting time is all I've done for over a hundred years."

With renewed determination, I studied the exhibits of faded, sepia tone photos from the local area and every example of memorabilia from a pickaxe to the badge that belonged Stagecoach's first sheriff.

I couldn't give up on Joshua. Even if it took the rest of my own earthly plane life, I would solve the mystery of his death.

NINE

After my unsettling visit to the museum and admonishing a puzzled Chester to take his vitamins, I'd paid a visit to the local library. Or rather, the tiny building with five rows of books to borrow and one filing cabinet of town history, including newspaper articles. It quickly became apparent that everything related to logging on the mountain had been copied directly from the library files.

That day had been exhausting, and all I really gained out of the trip was a clearer perspective of what Joshua's life must've been like back then. I certainly had faces to the names now, with both Lance and Sherman being on my asshole list.

The rest of the week had been spent doing various chores such as fixing the back porch railing, with Joshua as my guide. After smashing my thumb with the hammer more than once, I became rather cranky at my predicament. What's the point of having a guy around who can build a cabin from the ground up if he can't wield a hammer and saw in the material world?

"Why can't I accompany you to Los Angeles?"

Joshua regarded me with a frown as I packed my small rolling suitcase with enough stuff to make it through a few days with Ana. I didn't want to encourage her into thinking I was staying longer. Viv hadn't been at the shop all week, and I wanted to get back to Squirrel Cove as quickly as I could.

I glanced up from the pile of shirts I was choosing from. I needed at least one decent outfit for the studio, and another in case we went someplace nice for dinner. Too bad I couldn't indulge in a dose of retail therapy, but finances were still tight.

"First off, we don't even know if you can go that far. What if we cross some mysterious etheric border, and you can never come back?"

Joshua arched his eyebrows. "Are you worried you'll never see me again?"

"What?" I huffed. "No. I just..." Being friends with a guy from the other side could be so annoying at times. It certainly didn't make things easy. "Wouldn't it suck if you got stuck somewhere else? Someplace worse than the cabin?"

"I can't imagine anyplace worse than the spot I've been trapped in for almost a hundred and fifty years."

His words hit me like a punch to the chest, but I was determined to keep my dignity. "I assumed that the fact you could now converse with someone, *anyone*, was better than being eternally alone." I swallowed down the ridiculous tears that threatened then went back to packing with a vengeance, turning away so he couldn't see my reaction. "Clearly, I was wrong."

Joshua sighed. "I apologize, that came out wrong. Cate, look at me."

I hurled a pair of strappy sandals into my case, the light bounce against the pile of clothing not giving me much satisfaction. Steeling my expression, I faced Joshua.

"Don't worry about it. I was also going to mention that I don't want Ana to determine I've gone batty living up here alone and talking to myself. Chester thinking that was one thing, my best friend another."

Joshua plucked his beard. "That's a reasonable concern. What if we practice a one-sided conversation? I could talk, comment on random things, and you could listen without responding."

I crossed my arms with a smirk. "That sounds suspiciously like my marriage. No thanks."

His eyebrows dipped low. "I don't understand."

"Neither did my husband." I tightened my ponytail, tugging on it a bit too hard. "Never mind. You can join me if you like, but no talking when we're around other people. And..." I still couldn't shake the fear that he might disappear and never come back. Not that I was attached to him or anything, but I *did* want to solve the mystery of his death. "...to be honest, I don't get why you want to come along so badly. It's not as if we'll uncover any clues in L.A. that pertain to your past. Not only that, but I have no idea what the deal is with this ghost hunter situation."

"Ghost hunter?" Joshua's eyes widened a bit. "I thought you said your friend does the cosmetics for performers on a television show."

Joshua had long been a fan of TV, since my aunt had spent many hours in her later years with it playing. His favorites were Big Valley and Matlock. Aunt Sylvia had been pretty old school.

"That's correct. However, the name of the show is Real Ghostly Encounters." I fiddled with the handle of the suitcase. I'd been hoping we wouldn't need this conversation since I'd planned on going to L.A. without him. "It's about a team of ghost hunters investigating different places that are supposed to be haunted. Then they film what happens."

Joshua wrinkled his brow. "Why?"

I probably should've watched a couple of episodes to get a better grasp of what the show was like, but I'd had other things on my mind.

"I think mostly it's because they're trying to prove there's life after death."

"Hmm..." Joshua frowned again. "I don't like the sound of these people hunting ghosts. Do they banish them to another realm? I've heard of spiritualists doing such things."

"No, of course not." *I hope.* "And I'm fairly certain these guys aren't spiritualists. My daughter says they're supposedly psychic, but my guess would be we're talking about a bunch of dudes who've always been into spooky stuff."

"Yet, here *you* are." He lifted one eyebrow.

"Okay, fine." I threw my hands in the air. "I was mistaken. I was wrong, ghosts really *do* exist. But we need to focus for a sec." I brushed back a few stray hairs from my forehead. "I don't know anything about these guys, how legit they are. My suspicion has always been that it's a load of crap. However, in light of my recent indoctrination into the wild and wonderful world of psychic abilities and paranormal activity—I suppose it's possible they're the real deal."

"Why would that be a problem?" Joshua shrugged. "Perhaps they could help me out, give me some guidance. Especially since your friend, Viv, hasn't been available."

I winced. "Yeah...no. I don't think that's such a great idea. I really don't want anyone knowing I'm living with a hundred and fifty-year-old ghost lumberjack or that I can detect when someone's Death ticket is about to be punched."

Joshua straightened, his chest puffing out a bit. "I see. You're ashamed of me. You consider me to be of a lesser social standing and you'd prefer your friends and family not be aware of my existence."

"Huh?" Where did he come up with this stuff? "*No,* that's not it at all." I swiped my hand across my forehead, frustration eating at me. "It's not about you, it's about me. My best friend and my daughter are already concerned about my mental and emotional state after all the recent changes in my life. This will only add unnecessary fuel to that fire. In addition, people in general give purported psychics the side eye, and I'm seriously not in the mood to deal with that right now."

"I'm not sure what you mean about the sides of eyes, but I'm sure there will be those who revere you for your talents. After all, these ghost hunters have their own television show, so they must be quite beloved." Joshua nodded sagely. "From what I can tell, only the best people are allowed on TV."

I pinched the bridge of my nose. Getting a ghost from another era to grasp the enormous amount of changes in society since they'd kicked the bucket was near impossible.

"I could go on for days why that last sentence is so epically inaccurate, but that's not what's important right now." I let out an exhausted sigh. "I tell you what. Come with me to L.A., but not to the studio. Let me go there first and see what the deal is with the show before we chance you being around them."

I couldn't put my finger on it, but somehow, the idea of Joshua and the Real Ghostly Encounters investigators crossing paths put me on edge.

"All right, Cate. I can agree to that."

I smiled, the tension I'd been holding in my body finally easing up a bit.

"Thanks." I glanced at my almost-full suitcase. "But we'd better get going or else I'll hit traffic."

"Traffic?"

"It's brutal." I wondered how much of my time conversing with Joshua was going to involve bringing him up to speed on the ways of the current world. "I'll explain on the ride there."

ANA THREW OPEN the door then broke into a wide smile. "You made it! I was getting worried."

I dragged my suitcase across the threshold, pointedly ignoring Joshua. He was nearby, I could feel his energy, but he wasn't visible. This was our agreement. It was so much easier to resist the urge to communicate with him if he wasn't right there in front of me.

"There was an overturned semi on the 10. I was worried I'd run out of gas right there on the freeway."

Ana grabbed the handle of my suitcase. "Poor baby! I know what you need and it's already breathing on the kitchen counter."

I chuckled. "Do I have to tell you how weird that just sounded."

She batted her eyelashes. "It's wine, kiddo. A gorgeous Cab with a woodsy undertone and a hint of blackberry."

"If you say mouthfeel, we can no longer be friends."

Ana let out an inelegant snort. "Get into your jammies or sweats or whatever, and we'll sit out on the patio with the firepit."

I surveyed the pristine, chicly appointed rooms as we passed through them on the way to the guest room. The modern, open floorplan also included and upstairs with an amazing view of Century City, so maybe that's where Ana's husband was hanging out.

"Is Brock upstairs?"

She glanced over her shoulder. "No. Working late. They have to get the special effects done for the teaser of Grudge Match IV. It's supposed to be very scary."

"I didn't realize there were three other Grudge Matches." I squinched up my nose. "Scary *and* gory, I presume."

"Duh. Otherwise, what's the point?"

She and Brock had met on the set of an indie film ten years before, went to dinner after work, and had never been apart since. They were the classic example of two peas in a pod.

Once I unpacked my belongings, I whispered to Joshua to get out of the room so I could change. So far, not only hadn't there been an issue of him disappearing, but we'd had a nice chat in the car. I discovered more about his early life and was beginning to get a better grasp of his character.

He'd genuinely believed he was doing the right thing by Cordelia in coming west. His intention had been to provide her with the life she deserved, and he was willing to go through any hardship necessary to give her what she wanted. I didn't come out and say anything, but it irked the hell out of me that she so callously tossed him aside, then added insult to injury by marrying his brother.

I suppose I didn't actually know how callous she'd been, but I felt oddly protective of Joshua. He'd been sincere in his intentions, but I wasn't so sure about her.

Taking a sip of the woodsy Cabernet, I relaxed in the thickly padded patio chair, enjoying the warmth from the firepit. The temperature was rather mild overall, but it was still nice to have that toastiness, along with the relaxing glow.

Ana drained her glass then regarded me. "Have you spoken with Hailey?"

I took another sip of mine. I needed to keep my wits about me in case I started blurting out 'I see dead people'.

"I called her before I left, but she's pulling a double today and tomorrow, then she has a term paper she's working on." I sighed. "Next time."

Ana tapped a pointy fingernail against her empty glass. "It must be hard. Not seeing her all the time, I mean. I'm probably not the best sympathizer since I've never had kids. All I can relate to is not wanting to hang out with my parents at all once I hit twelve." She shrugged. "And it's never changed."

I frowned. "Thanks for that."

She covered her mouth with one hand, then held it out for my glass. "Sorry, wasn't thinking. Top you off?"

I glanced at my still mostly full drink. "No, I'm good. That drive sucked the life out of me. If I drink too much, I'll never make it out of bed in the morning." I shifted on the chair trying to find a casual way to bring up the topic of the show. "So...the show."

Ana arched her eyebrows. "The show? Or Stan's death? Don't even try to pretend like you care about the supernatural all of a sudden."

"Well..." This was going to be about as difficult as I thought it would be. "You know me. Always inquisitive." I fought to keep my tone off-hand and casual. "And since I'm going to hang out with psychics and specters, I might as well embrace the vibe."

Ana grabbed the neck of the wine bottle then poured the contents into her glass until it was full. "You're up to something. I can sense it." After taking a healthy swallow of her drink, she shrugged. "I won't harass you over whatever scheme you've got brewing, as long as you inform me immediately of any juicy gossip. Deal?"

"I can live with that." I licked my lips, daring to press forward. "But tell me truthfully. What's your take on this Dirk guy, in terms of his psychic prowess? Do you honestly believe he's interacting with the undead?"

Ana scrunched up her nose. "Hard to say. If nothing else, he's super believable when he says he hears a voice or sees an apparition. Even though Stan wouldn't admit it—because science—I would've bet on him being more spiritually gifted over Dirk."

This was exactly what I needed to know. As far as I was concerned, the less psychic Dirk was, the better. I didn't want him messing with Joshua.

"How so?"

Ana leaned forward, dropping her voice conspiratorially. "Don't say one word of this while you're on set. But he gets all weird and dramatic sometimes when he has a so-called encounter. Some of the low-rent actors we hire for the re-enactments are more likely to get an Emmy than him."

I arched my eyebrows. "In other words, you think he's a big faker."

Ana shushed me. "I didn't say *that*. Just that he goes overboard. For all I know, he sees a ghost, thinks it's yawn-worthy after all these years of investigating, but feels he has to play it up for the camera."

"Hmm." She wasn't helping. "Okay," I said. "What about the evidence. I mean, the investigators get evidence, right? Isn't that the point of their whole dog and pony show?"

Ana pursed her lips. "Funny. And yeah, they get what you could call evidence."

"Is there something else you'd call it?"

Ana groaned. "I don't know. They get recordings of sounds and voices, or mumbling, or whatever. Sometimes there will be a loud bang or strange lights and shadows that they get on film. That sort of thing."

At the mention of strange shadows, I shuddered. *No thanks.* Didn't need to see that again.

"That doesn't sound all that amazing. They've built an entire show around unexplained noises and lights?"

With what I'd been dealing with lately, I wondered if I should start my own damn show.

Ana took a noisy sip of her wine. "There's the occasional, more shocking moment. Like, one time a bunch of books came flying off the shelves behind Dirk. Oh, and there was another time when there was this ghastly, unexplained scream that made one of the sound guys pee himself. That was hella creepy." She drained her glass. "I was pretty bummed out, though, since I was in the trailer when it happened."

"Wow." Maybe Dirk was in tune with the other side after all. "Has he ever tried to, you know, exorcise any of the ghosts?"

Ana rolled her eyes. "Seriously, Cate? The dude's not a priest."

I shrugged. "I don't know all the protocol of this stuff. I'm only trying to figure out his endgame. I mean, after he encounters the ghosts, records the ghosts, and speaks to the ghosts—does he try to get rid of them somehow?"

"Honey, I think the endgame is more seasons. They try to change it up by bringing on guest investigators and traveling to notorious murder sites where there are rumors of spirits. But beyond that, I don't think Dirk or the producers care what happens to these poor, sad, dead people."

A burst of anger flared through me. How could they treat people that way? These were real souls who were trapped against their will on this earthly plane. Of course, I couldn't speak for all ghosts. Maybe some didn't want to leave.

I sighed. I couldn't save the ghost world, but for some reason, I'd been chosen to save Joshua.

And that's exactly what I planned to do.

CHAPTER

TEN

The morning was a challenge. Joshua started in on me first thing, insisting he should come with me to the studio. I still couldn't shake the feeling that him crossing paths with the ghost investigation team was a horrible idea, so I'd ended up bargaining with him. He could come to dinner with me and Ana that night if he cooled his jets at her house while I was at the studio.

Then I explained what cooling his jets meant.

Bargaining with him was easy—at least for now. Everything was a new adventure after being confined to approximately seven hundred square feet for over a century. Even if he couldn't eat the food, merely getting to be somewhere new and different was a thrill.

Once I'd settled that dilemma, I rode with Ana to the studio with the sun barely cracking the horizon. I was now sitting in an empty chair next to the makeup trailer, waiting while Ana worked on the performers.

So far, I'd only seen one guy go inside the trailer, and I had no idea who he was. I knew what Dirk and Stan looked like. Although, I was hoping I *wouldn't* see Stan. But as far as the rest of the people connected with the show, I was clueless.

I took a sip of the supposedly amazing organic brew that the executive producer insisted the craft service provide, grateful that it was at least hot. I figured that producer and I simply weren't cut from the same cloth. In my imagination, mud tasted better than this dreck.

"Hey, are you waiting for Ana?"

A woman with tortoise shell rimmed glasses, a perky nose—and annoyingly bright smile for so early in the morning—stared down at me.

I shifted in the uncomfortable chair, my joints protesting at not moving and being in the same spot for so long.

"In a manner of speaking. I'm her friend, Cate." I glanced around. "Am I in the way here?"

She gestured with her hand, waving off my concerns. "Oh no, not at all. I'm one of the production assistants, and I've been trying to track down the woman doing a car crash reenactment. Long story." She held out her hand. "Anyway, I'm Ronnie. Nice to meet you. If you see a woman about your age wandering around, tell her to get into makeup immediately, then report to me. I'll be in the soundstage."

I pointed to one of the enormous, non-descript white buildings. "It's the one with the number five on it, right?"

"Yeah." She leaned down, covering one side of her mouth with her hand. "Stay away from six. It's a closed set today because they're filming a pretty graphic sex scene. At least, that's the gossip going around."

My ears pricked up, and not because of the sex scene. *Gossip.* The so-called accidental death of Stan came to mind.

"Good to know. And I'll definitely keep an eye out for her."

"Thanks. I'd better get back. The director is ready to do the first shot that opens up the new season."

I had to make my move. "Sure, uh, is that the segment where Dirk talks about how sad everyone is over Stan's death?"

My delivery could've been more delicate, but I'd been caught unaware.

"It is." She shifted on her feet. "I'm sure Ana mentioned he wasn't all that popular, but it doesn't mean we're all glad he's dead."

"Wha—?" Oh man, I shouldn't have blurted. Not only was I a terrible psychic so far, I was a dismal fail as a sleuth as well. I hoped I hadn't just created a problem for Ana. "No, I didn't mean that. She might've mentioned something about wondering if I'd seen the news, that sort of thing."

Ronnie shook her head. "I'm not worried about what Ana said, we've all been floating theories on what really happened to him. But personally, I was starting to feel sort of malicious about it." She shrugged. "It's hard to know how to feel when someone's been so evil to everyone, and even harder not to assume that someone did him in."

My eyebrows shot up. "Evil? So, you're saying that it seems as if someone might've murdered him?"

"Oh yeah, totally." She let out a snort. "Stan took himself and his metaphysical research *way* too seriously. No one was a smart or as awesome as he was. He treated everyone around him as if they were complete idiots. And if he decided you weren't giving his field of science the respect it deserved? He ripped you a new one. I can't tell you how many directors, actors, writers—even this macho stuntman who did one of the re-enactments left the set in tears."

"Damn." I considered her words. "But doesn't it seem sort of extreme to murder someone because they're a jerk?" I chuckled. "I mean, sure, we've all had our moments where we've blurted out that we wanted to kill someone, but we don't actually *do* it."

Ronnie nodded. "Of course. But…" She leaned down, glancing around like she was checking if anyone was nearby before speaking. "There are a few people who some of us on the crew feel had more than enough reasons to take him out."

"Really?" I was trying not to vibrate with excitement. It was nice to know that the suspect list could be narrowed down from half the planet to a choice few. "Like who?"

Ronnie looked around again then squatted next to the chair. She kept her voice low. "I totally shouldn't be telling you this, but the current list includes the executive producer, Stan's would've been ex-wife if he hadn't died so suddenly, her mystery lover, and Dirk."

I gasped before I could stop myself. "Dirk? Wouldn't he be taking a chance the show got cancelled and he was out of a job?"

"That almost happened, so you're not off-track there. However, there's been so much bad blood between them the past few years, it's plausible Dirk could've just lost it on him one night."

"Fair enough." I scraped my teeth along my bottom lip. "Which means Dirk could've impulsively pushed him down the mine shaft as opposed to planning it out."

Ronnie shrugged again. "Could be. Although, it's sort of backwards in the sense that Stan was super jealous of all the attention Dirk was getting. He felt that Dirk didn't care about discovering evidence of hauntings as much as he enjoyed playing up to the camera and his fans." She chuckled. "Dirk's social media game is on point."

"Right…"

A crime of passion sounded plausible. In particular, because it would've been so easy in a moment of rage to react without thinking, to give poor Stan a push to his doom. Which also might mean that Dirk hadn't meant to kill him, that it was merely an awful accident.

"Well..." Ronnie rose to her feet. "I need to get going. They're probably ready to start shooting."

I wanted to interject that she hadn't given me the current theories of why the wife and executive producer wanted the despised Stan dead, but figured I was pushing my luck as it was. Maybe I'd run into her later, or maybe I'd overhear some gossip from other crew members. Then there was always Ana. Who knew? She could pick up a few tidbits herself over the course of the long day.

"Sure, I don't want to keep you." I smiled up at her. "It was nice meeting you."

"You too." Ronnie's face lit up, her cheery grin back in place. "I'm sure I'll see you later."

After Ronnie left, I pondered everything she'd told me. The curiosity over what the executive producer and the wife's motives might be gnawed at me. Then there was the mystery lover. What was that all about?

"Hey, girl," said Ana as she descended from the trailer. "Bored out of your mind yet?"

I rose from the chair, still clutching my half-full cup of now-cool coffee. "Let me get this straight. You invited me to drive over a hundred miles so I could be bored out of my mind with you instead of at home?"

"Of course." She jerked her head toward the soundstage. "At least here, you're not alone."

If only she knew how un-alone I was.

ANA HADN'T BEEN KIDDING about the boredom factor. Every shot took forever with multiple people stopping to adjust lights or touch up make-up or discuss what was happening in the segment. I'd been so intent on solving a murder, I hadn't thought to bring something to read, and the rules on the set demanded that all phones be shut off.

There had been one interesting development, though. Dirk hadn't shown up to film his segment on Stan, so the director had been hastily pulling in the other cast members in the meantime. The crew was abuzz as to why he wasn't there, with wild rumors going around that maybe someone had killed him too. That led to whisperings that perhaps the entire cast was in danger.

Clearly, the crew was as bored as me.

"There he is!" whispered Ronnie to another PA.

I hadn't caught the other production assistant's name, but she seemed the most enthusiastic when it came to gossip. I'd made sure to strategically position my chair near the area she tended to hover over.

As Dirk breezed in, he kept his head ducked, seemingly careful not to make eye contact with anyone. He moved across the set as if he was on a mission, his hurried strides leading him directly to the director's side. They engaged in a brief, intense discussion, but it didn't appear as though the director was mad. If I had to guess, his demeanor radiated concern more than anything.

"Okay, people," yelled out Sam, the director. "We're taking thirty while Mr. Peterson gets ready for his scene. Be back on time, we still have a lot to get through today."

The gangly, young co-investigator who'd been in the middle of his tearful Stan memorial speech appeared perplexed. He was coaxed off the set by the crew who was anxious to reposition everything for Dirk. I might not know all that much about the show, but I didn't doubt for a minute that it revolved around Dirk.

I stood, stretching my arms above my head, trying to act nonchalant as I edged closer to the same group of crew members who'd been whispering to each other all morning. I casually leaned over the snack table under the pretense of examining the donut selection. While I didn't mean to bump elbows with anyone, it did give me a reason to speak to them.

"Oh, sorry!" I laughed shakily. "Didn't mean to run into you like that."

"I'll survive."

The man whose personal space I'd invaded gave me a wide smile, as sincere as the one Ronnie had given me when we met that morning. For all the drama they had suffered through, the crew seemed rather sunny in disposition. I hated to think it, but maybe Stan's demise made the work environment less hostile.

I cleared my throat, not wanting to end the conversation. Most of the time was spent with everyone remaining stone cold silent while they filmed, so this was a rare moment to interact.

"I'm Cate, by the way." I hooked my thumb over my shoulder toward the makeup trailer. "I'm Ana's guest today."

A woman who couldn't be a day older than my daughter peered over the man's shoulder. Although, everyone seemed way younger than me these days.

"Oh yeah, Ana's told me about you." She stuck her hand over the guy's shoulder with him pursing his lips at her. "I'm Tasha, the hair stylist. Ana and I go way back in the industry."

"Um, excuse me," said the poor guy she was still leaning over. "I'm not a prop, you know." He batted his lashes at me. "Although I do handle quite a few of them. I'm Eric, the prop assistant."

I chuckled. "Nice to meet you both."

Although I'd accepted Tasha's hand, I'd let go of it as quickly as I could. I doubted this young woman had any shadow people creeping up on her, but I didn't want to find out if she did.

"So..." I plucked a napkin from the table, dragging out the process of choosing a pastry as long as possible. Randomly standing at the table for no reason seemed questionable. "I wonder why Dirk showed up so late? I hope he's okay."

Tasha rolled her eyes. "Ah, I get it. You're one of those."

My fingers had almost landed on a cruller, then I froze. "One of those what?"

Tasha and Eric both giggled, but Eric was the one who answered. "His groupies. Now we know why you got Ana to bring you along today."

"Huh?" I shook my head vehemently. "No, I—"

"This is a good day for that," Tasha interjected. "Things are usually too crazy when we do the night shoots for the investigations, and no one is really allowed to be there except the mobile crew." Eric and Tasha shared a solemn nod.

Could their misinterpretation work to my advantage?

"You got me." I laughed harder this time. "He's a real hunk, all right."

Did people still say that? I hadn't thought about hunks in forever. I certainly hadn't been around any, either. *Although...* My cheeks heated as my thoughts strayed to Joshua.

Eric groaned. "Tell me about it. It's kills me how straight he is."

Tasha snorted and elbowed him in the ribs. "Better than *him* killing you."

Eric gasped. "Shut your mouth." He regarded me. "Don't listen to her. If anyone offed Stan, it was his wife." He curled his lip. "That shameless hussy."

I steeled my expression, hoping I was exuding great sincerity. "I couldn't agree more. Dirk couldn't have done it. He's such a..." *Damn.* I had no idea what he was or wasn't. "Hot guy."

Eric threw his hands in the air. "Right? No way would he risk his career and fans and all that fabulousness by killing Stan. Elliot wanted to dump him anyway. It wouldn't make sense for Dirk to take that chance." He shrugged. "All he had to do was wait it out."

I was practically salivating from the outpouring of juicy gossip. I'd even lost interest in the cruller.

"Who's Elliot?"

"Sorry," Eric laughed. "Elliot Vance, the executive producer. He's a total control freak and Stan was simply a freak all the way around. Those two were the proverbial oil and water together."

Tasha stuck her head between me and Eric as if we were all conspiring to commit a murder of our own. "Elliot was the one who encouraged Dirk to steal the spotlight from Stan. He knows a ratings cash cow when he sees one."

Eric pointed to Tasha and nodded. "What she said. Whenever the camera was on Stan during an investigation, it was a huge snooze fest. Amiright?"

Tasha laughed. "For real. Like, blah blah blah, I'm a science god, blah, blah, four syllable words, blah, who cares."

"Wow." I hadn't realized so much drama and intrigue could be packed into one, vaguely popular, ghost investigation show. "What about the shameless hussy?" I slapped a hand over my mouth. "I mean, his wife?"

Tasha's eyes widened and Eric made a slicing motion across his throat. I squinted at them, trying to determine what secret code they were communicating in as they continued to make odd, clipped gestures and twist their faces into bizarre expressions. I wasn't sure if they were trying to tell me something, or if they were in pain.

"Hey, guys. Mind if I squeeze in here?"

I whirled around at the sound of the deep-timbred voice, and locked eyes with the man himself, Dirk Peterson.

"Uh, s-sure," I sputtered. "I'll just get out of your way." I scooched backward, and Eric let out a yell as I stomped on his toe. "Sorry." I winced. "I can see I'm causing a problem, so if you'll all excuse me—"

"Hold up." Dirk pointed a finger at me. "Are you new this season?" In keeping with everyone else I'd met so far, his smile seemed genuine. "I like to make it a habit of knowing all the crewmembers." A shadow crossed his features. "It feels even more important after what happened to Stan. I've always thought of this show as home, and everyone working here as family." He lowered his head. "I still can't believe he's gone."

And *I* couldn't tell if he was practicing his speech for the camera, or if he genuinely meant what he said. Either way, it felt off for him to say it to a complete stranger.

"I'm so sorry for your loss."

My words were sincere. I might be suspicious of the guy, but I didn't know the real Dirk. And I certainly didn't know if he'd killed his friend and partner. I also decided to take that moment to remind myself that Stan's death hadn't been ruled a homicide.

"Thank you." Dirk's smile came back, and he sandwiched my hand between his own. "I'm so glad someone as kind-hearted as you has joined our little family."

Cotton filled my ears the moment our hands touched, and only the muffled sounds of Eric and Tasha speaking over each other could be heard. My head seemed heavy, as if I couldn't support the weight of it on my neck, and for a moment, I thought I might collapse to the ground. The second Dirk released my hand, the sensations all vanished in a whoosh.

I blinked rapidly. *That was weird.* At least there hadn't been dark figures of doom added to the equation.

Dirk tilted his head. "Are you okay, Cate?"

My jaw dropped. "How did you know my name?"

Dirk regarded me like I'd lost my mind while both Eric and Tasha burst out laughing.

"Honey," said Eric. "We just introduced you five seconds ago, remember?" He and Tasha exchanged glances with a smirk. "As I was saying, Dirk, Cate is Ana's friend."

Dirk appeared confused for a second then broke into a smile again. "Oh right, Ana. She's the makeup girl."

I arched my eyebrows. Dirk's life expectancy would be severely shortened if Ana ever heard him refer to her as a girl.

"Yup, she's a close friend and invited me to be here today."

Dirk's gaze traveled down my frame then up again. Had I just been visually fondled? It had been a minute since anyone had looked at me that way, so I couldn't be sure.

Dirk winked. "I'll have to thank her later." Before I could react, he broke eye contact and grabbed the cruller I'd been plotting on. "Time for me to head back in. Nice meeting you Cate."

I smiled, thankful that he was juggling the donut and a cup of coffee, instead of reaching out to touch me again. "It was great meeting you, too."

As soon as he disappeared into the recesses of the soundstage, both Eric and Tasha started squealing, each of them shaking one of my arms.

"Whoa, take it easy guys." It was a good thing I wasn't holding a cup of coffee of my own.

"Oh my God, Cate." Eric was still squeezing the life out of my arm. "I can tell he's totally into you."

Tasha barked out a laugh. "But you almost gave yourself away by staring at him with that dazed expression on your face."

Eric patted my back. "Honey, you can't be that obvious. You gotta play not quite, but sort of, hard to get."

"Oh, I..." Uh-oh. Maybe his visual inspection was as inappropriate as I'd thought it was. "Really?"

Eric nodded. "This is *so* exciting. If I can't have him, I'm glad it's you."

I shook my head in disbelief. "Uh, I don't think it's time to run out and start picking out china patterns quite yet. I shared all of two or three generic sentences with the man."

Tasha whacked Eric on the side of his arm. "Yeah. She barely knows the guy, and besides, he might be a murderer."

Eric squinched up his nose. "True. I hadn't thought of that."

While they continued to debate whether I should risk my life by dating the hot reality star of Eric's dreams, Joshua entered my thoughts. I couldn't help but wonder what he'd think of the whole situation.

I quickly nabbed a maple bar and pretended to be incredibly interested in what Tasha and Eric were discussing. Meanwhile, I thanked whoever those fates were that Viv kept mentioning for giving me the foresight to leave Joshua at Ana's place.

I had a feeling he wouldn't be as thrilled about Dirk's interest in me as my new friends were.

CHAPTER

ELEVEN

"Oh my God." Ana kicked off her flats then plopped down on the enormous blue sectional of her living room, resting her feet on the cushions, and leaning against the sofa arm. "What a bizarre day. Not only did I have to hurry and do Dirk's makeup when he finally appeared, but then I had to redo everyone else who was going to take his place when he didn't show.

She stretched and yawned. "I know I said we'd go out, but I'm beat. Is it cool if we order in?"

"Sure, I'm fine with that." Ordering in didn't exist in Squirrel Cove, so it was a treat in its own way. "I'd be up for some Thai."

Her head lolled in my direction. "Not much in the way of cuisine variety on the mountain?"

I felt strangely defensive of my new little town. "There are choices. Just not that one."

As soon as we called in our order, we both changed out of our all-day-at-the-studio clothes. I had to give Ana credit. She worked long, hard hours when she was contracted for a shoot, and from what I'd picked up from the other crew members, everyone thought she was top notch.

Before I headed back to the living room to join Ana, I thought I should touch base with Joshua. He'd been sort of butt hurt when I left that morning, trying to give me a last-ditch reason why he should go. As it turned out, he was kind of right.

There hadn't been any ghostly goings-on and if Dirk was some sort of psychic or empath or sensitive when it came to spirits, I hadn't picked up on it. Then again, I was hardly the eighth psychic wonder of the world, so for all I knew, he was seeing ghosts right and left, but was merely used to it.

"Psst, Joshua," I whispered. "Are you around?"

I waited, almost ninety percent sure he couldn't go anywhere without me. I'd left the pendant behind, because I had the feeling if I wore it, the decision of whether he would come with me or not would be out of our hands. But what if I'd goofed and he'd been thrust back to the cabin, or worse, banished into some void where I'd never see him again?

"Are you decent, Cate?"

I exhaled with so much relief I sounded like a balloon rapidly losing air. "Definitely decent." He appeared before me. "Any problems while I was gone? I wasn't sure what to expect when I got back."

Joshua pursed his lips. "You were right, it was exactly as you predicted."

"Don't sound so insulted."

He averted his gaze. "It has nothing to do with being insulted. I would simply prefer not to be bossed around all the time."

I gasped. "Bossed around? *Excuse* me?"

My voice had ticked up several notches in both tone and volume. I needed to dial it back before Ana busted me.

Joshua crossed his arms and still wouldn't meet my eyes.

I stamped my foot. Something about the man brought out my inner four-year-old. "What?"

His gaze traveled to the ceiling. "Oh nothing. Just that I've been wandering around this ugly white house all day with nothing to do, no one to talk to."

"Ugly white house? Seriously?"

Joshua sighed. "Cate, please understand. I'm filled with gratitude that you're allowing my troubles to take up so much of your life..."

I held in a snort. *I have a life?* Thankfully, Joshua didn't read minds.

He continued, "But the frustration over being controlled by these invisible boundaries, of not being allowed to come and go as I please..." He sighed again. "What I'm trying to say is that any opportunity to go somewhere I haven't been since my passing, or to not be alone, isn't something I want to miss."

I hung my head. I know I'd be frustrated beyond all reason as well.

Lifting my gaze, I locked eyes with him. "Being bossy isn't my intention, okay? I'm serious when I say I'm not much of a psychic, that I pretty much have no clue what I'm doing. What if that Dirk guy saw you and, I don't know, messed with you somehow?"

Joshua pressed his lips together, nodding. "Yes, I know. I suppose it's that I'm not going back into my dormant state—or whatever you want to call it—like I used to. Since you began wearing the pendant, I experience everything in real time again."

"Oh." I hadn't considered that. "Even today when I wasn't wearing it?"

"Yes." He arched his eyebrows. "You don't wear it all the time. Remember? There was that one time after you showered then went to the market, and you forgot to put it back on."

I frowned. "You better not have firsthand knowledge of that shower."

He peered down his nose at me. "As I've said repeatedly, I'm a gentleman."

"See that you remain that way." We shared a brief, not too aggressive, scowl before I continued. "Regardless, I assumed you stayed at the cabin like you always do. Nothing was different about that."

"Except that time passed like it does on your plane. It thought it odd but decided to hold off mentioning it until there was more of an explicit example. I think how today played out accomplished that objective."

I considered his words. Two aspects of the pendant's power over us came to mind. Or more accurately, my power over him. I hated to admit it to myself, but I could control him by not wearing the pendant and leaving him behind whenever I felt like it.

But this new knowledge also made my responsibility to Joshua much heavier on my shoulders. If his life after death was no longer limited to brief interactions with the living, then what would Joshua do with all the endless hours he was now aware of? There were only so many reruns of Matlock a person could watch.

"Wow." I wasn't sure what else to say. "On the plus side, now that I've checked out the situation on the set, I'll feel more comfortable having you along if I ever go back again."

Joshua's jaw dropped. "You're not going back? What about that murder you said you wanted to solve?"

I had to laugh. He sounded disappointed that he wouldn't be with me while we searched for clues.

"I'm still curious about Stan's death, it's not that. Mostly it's because Ana has these long, grueling days ahead of her for a while, so we can't really hang out after she gets off work. What they're doing right now at the studio is super boring, at least to me."

"What's boring about it?" He shrugged. "You could probably pick up some ghost hunting pointers we can use in my situation."

"Which would be awesome if there was any actual investigating going on. They're trying to do as much of the studio stuff at one time before they go on location for the actual hunting of the ghosts."

"Hmm..." Joshua tugged on his beard. "Will you be able to go one of the locations?"

I'd been waiting to drop this bomb on him. "Funny you should mention that. I've already asked Ana, and she thinks she can finagle it because I was so well behaved on the set today, and..." I cleared my throat. "Well, I guess Dirk took a liking to me."

Joshua's interested expression instantly morphed into a glare. "I see. And how, pray tell, did that come about?"

I rubbed the back of my neck, not sure why this conversation made me so uncomfortable. "Over the snack table."

His eyebrows dipped low. "*Snack* table?"

"Yes. At the set they have an area where you can..." I huffed. "Never mind. Basically, I was speaking to two crew members during a break, and he just happened to wander over."

Joshua muttered something unintelligible. I leaned forward, tilting my head.

"What was that?"

Joshua stuck his chin in the air. "Nothing important. What were you saying about the location?"

I narrowed my eyes, wondering what was bothering him. "I was *saying* that normally they don't allow guests while they're filming the investigations, but it would be okay for me to go one night."

"I see." His tone remained clipped. "And when is this happening?"

Now I was fighting not to roll my eyes. "I'm not sure. But I was thinking about checking out the mine shaft that Stan fell in. That was where they were supposed to film the first show of the season initially, but decided to pick somewhere else nearby instead." I wrinkled my nose. "You know, since it would be in such poor taste to go ahead with the original location."

"I don't know about that," commented Joshua. "I would think that investigating the mine shaft would present the perfect opportunity to discover what happened to Stan." He chuckled. "After all, they're a ghost hunting show and Stan is surely a ghost by now." The corner of Joshua's mouth quirked. "Unless he's luckier than me and was able to move on."

I held up my finger. "I'm way ahead of you. I was thinking that if you came with me, you might be able to communicate with Stan, or get an idea of what happened to him. Because that's my theory as to why they cancelled the filming there. I'm betting that whoever killed Stan is thinking the same thing, that Stan will show up and out them somehow."

Joshua grinned, his sour expression turning to one of excitement. "Exactly. When can we go?"

"Hold on there, turbo. I'm half-dead from today, it's nighttime, and my dinner is almost here. This is an undertaking for another day."

Joshua growled in what seemed like frustration. "I suppose. Carry on," He smirked at me. "And I certainly hope you're not being literal when you say you're half dead. I need someone who has my interests at heart on your side of the etheric veil."

I smirked back. "Thanks for your concern." The doorbell rang and I glanced over my shoulder. "That's my green curry." I turned to leave then paused, regarding Joshua again. "Um, come hang out with us if you want. Just, you know. Don't talk to me. Ana's already worried about me being in the mountains all alone, and I'm so tired I'll probably blurt that you're right there next to me."

Joshua smiled. "I'll be even quieter than a mouse."

"That's good. Because those mice at the cabin need to shut up when I'm sleeping. All that scurrying around is getting on my nerves."

Joshua followed me as I headed down the hall. "Maybe I can scare them off for you since I don't sleep. Can mice see ghosts?"

I chuckled. "I have no idea. Go for it."

By the time we reached the kitchen where Ana was removing the takeout cartons from the bag, Joshua had fallen silent. I felt a twinge in my chest. Maybe someday, somehow, Ana would get to meet him. I was certain they'd get along great.

Ana suggested we eat outside by the firepit, which sounded wonderful to me. We opened a bottle of wine, a sort of ritual with us when we stayed in, choosing a white Zinfandel this time. Ana's silence while we devoured our food spoke to how exhausted she truly was.

I wondered if I should hold off on grilling her about all I'd learned that day, but she seemed to rally after consuming a pile of pad Thai and two chicken satay skewers.

"Ugh." She pushed her plate away. "I never ate one thing today." She tipped back her glass and drained the last of her wine. "Wait, I'm lying. I had a handful of gummy bears. Oh, and a couple bites of a stale donut around three."

"Yummy." I didn't confess that I'd managed to do my share of donut annihilation throughout the day. The key was to only take one at a time and leave long spaces between trips to the food table. "You didn't get a lunch break?"

We'd spent almost no time together in the twelve hours we'd been at the studio.

"According to Union rules, I did. According to everything I needed to handle, I didn't."

"You can't complain?"

"I can totally complain. They'd just tell me to take my break."

"But get angry if you don't do everything they expect of you."

She tipped her refilled glass at me. "Welcome to show business."

In truth, I'd gone through similar scenarios at the random, dead-end jobs I'd held over the years. Managers who admonished me for not taking my state mandated breaks, then admonishing me even harsher for falling behind on a task that three people should've been performing in the first place.

I sighed and guzzled—*sipped*—my wine. A comfortable silence filled the space between us. The decades of knowing each other and growing closer helped us discover we were true sisters in spirit.

After a few minutes, Ana broke the quiet of the cool evening. "That was crazy with Dirk today, though. It almost made the grueling day worth it."

Excellent. A valid opening. "Yeah, I was curious about that. Why was he late?"

"Oh, I thought you heard. I spotted you hanging out with Eric and Tasha. They couldn't keep their mouths shut if their lips were coated in super glue."

I snort-chuckled. "I didn't mind. They were fun and it's no big secret that my inner amateur sleuth is curious about Stan's so-called accident."

Ana gave me a wry smile. "Yeah. I might've picked up on that. Anyway, Dirk told Jim—the director—that he was run off the road when he drove over the hill on Laurel Canyon. One of the gaffers overheard the conversation and told Ronnie who then told me. I figured the story had made it around the entire set by noon."

"Really? Huh. That's an interesting development."

Had the person—or persons—who killed Stan, also set their sights on Dirk? Or had he faked it to divert suspicion?

"And get this," Ana continued. "Apparently, the show's been getting hate mail from an extreme religious group, saying the investigators are all instruments of the devil. No one made a specific threat on their lives, but it does make you think."

A stab of guilt hit me. Here I was thinking the murderer could be one of Stan's friends, *wife* even, but his death might have nothing to do with them.

And, it might still only be an unfortunate accident.

I rubbed my finger along my upper lip, my mind whirling with all the possibilities. I regarded Ana.

"What do *you* think? You're closer to the situation, know the people involved much better than I do. All gossip aside, do you honestly believe any of the suspects the crew are gossiping about could be capable of murder?"

Ana twirled the stem of her glass between her fingers. "Anyone's capable of anything."

I frowned. "You don't honestly believe *that*, do you? I can't envision a scenario where I could actually *murder* someone. I don't believe that for a second about you, either. Especially a person you have a relationship with."

Ana shook her head. "I'm not saying either of us are currently of a mind to kill anyone. Although, there are a few actors I've worked with through the years who I wouldn't cry over if they fell down a mine shaft." She set down her empty glass. "But what I'm getting at, is how well do we really know what someone is capable of? I certainly don't have special insight into what Dirk, Lily or Elliot might do if pushed against a wall."

"Lily's the wife?"

Ana nodded. "You mean no one smack-talked her today? That's a shocker."

"Oh, they did. But I was beginning to think the name on her birth certificate was Shameless Hussy."

Ana choked on her wine. "That sounds like the crew. It's because she was supposedly having an affair with the pool boy, her tennis coach and..." She tapped a finger to her lip. "Some actor. I forget."

"Yikes. Why didn't she just divorce the guy?"

"Money, honey." She rubbed her thumb and fingers together. "Stan had mucho dinero. Which brings me back to the fact that no one really knows what someone else is capable of."

She had a point. Despite all the murder mysteries and true crime shows and books I'd partaken of over the years, I still found myself shocked when a person killed someone close to them.

"I see where you're coming from." I considered finishing up the last of my wine, then reconsidered. I was pretty beat and wanted to get an early start in the morning. "I'm just so intrigued by it all."

"I'm rather intrigued as well, but about something else entirely."

Ana's grin told me she was up to something. I narrowed my eyes at her.

"What are you getting at?"

"Oh, I don't know." Ana brushed her hand through the air. "Just that I might have spotted a certain sexy ghost hunter making googly eyes at my best friend. I considered giving him a cup to catch the drool but thought that might be overkill."

"Gross!"

Ana slapped a palm to her chest. "How can you say such a thing. I know muscle hunks aren't everyone's jam, but I don't think Dirk is gross."

"I wasn't referring to Dirk," I huffed. "I meant your remark about the drool. But never mind that. More importantly, I want to go on record and say that Dirk most certainly was *not* making googly eyes."

I pretended not to remember his visual come on from when we met earlier.

Ana rolled her eyes. "Whatever. I saw what I saw. Why not

simply enjoy the validation of a young, handsome celebrity having a crush on you?"

I've always heard that it's not a good idea to mix Tylenol with booze, but rules were meant to be broken.

"I'm not even going to get into why I don't need any validation from a guy—handsome or not."

Ana gave me a quick nod. "You're right, you don't. I could've worded that better. I guess what I was getting at, is I know how devastated you were about Vince shacking up with Miss Super-model." She sighed. "I know you're not into casual hook-ups. But holy guacamole, think what an ego boost it would be to bone a famous heartthrob. Plus, he's a total man-whore, so you won't have to worry about him wanting a relationship."

Tylenol for sure. "Ana. Enough. I know your intentions are good, but I don't want my first post-divorce *interlude* to be with a man-whore."

She let out a dramatic sigh. "Okay, just sayin'. Anyway, you might change your mind when they begin filming in Squirrel Cove next week."

I gasped, almost falling out of my chair. "*What*? When did that come about?"

Ana laughed. "Oh my God, your face."

"You mean you're messing with me?"

She shook her head. "Nope. It's for real. And I've known for a while it was a possibility, but it wasn't verified until this afternoon. I guess they were waiting for permission to film at the Mountain Wildlife Center."

I drew my eyebrows together. "The Wildlife Center? What's supposed to be there?" I snorted. "Coyote ghosts? Haunted trees?"

"To be honest, I don't follow all the details of these episodes. Some of them are so yawn-worthy because nothing much really happens. They try to fill the time with chills and thrills that the investigators are supposedly experiencing. Not that it matters, since people tune in to swoon over Dirk anyway." She smirked. "Hence the reason Stan was so pissed off about the direction the show was taking."

"Yeah, but there has to be *some* reason to film a ghost show there. I doubt they're randomly dragging everyone up to the mountains for laughs."

Ana grunted. "I wish. From what I gather, you're not too far off with the tree thing. Something about a lumberjack from the eighteen hundreds who was murdered by the owner of the logging company."

The blood seemed to drain from my body, my limbs turning to jelly. "M-murdered?"

Ana frowned. "Yeah. Murdered. You know, your favorite topic?"

I wasn't so sure about that anymore.

TWELVE

I hadn't slept one bit the night before. All I could visualize was poor Joshua being killed for some unknown reason, deprived of the chance to make a new life for himself after Cordelia's betrayal.

It's so unfair.

As I unpacked my clothes, tossing everything I'd worn into the laundry basket, I attempted to push aside the depressing thoughts. As it was, I regretted inviting Joshua to hang out with me and Ana after the big murder bombshell she'd dropped.

Poor Joshua. We hadn't discussed Ana's revelation yet and he'd been so sullen on the drive home, I didn't want to bring up the subject. The ride to L.A. had been much jollier, with me as the unofficial tour guide while he excitedly took in all the new and strange sights of modern life.

To help add to my frustration, Ana didn't have any details regarding the haunting or the murder. Her disinterest in the particulars of the episodes was irking the hell out of me. Being blind-sided by the show and my continuing fear over whether Dirk might have the ability to interact with Joshua in a negative way had me on edge.

More than ever, I needed to see Viv.

After shoving my empty suitcase into the back of the closet, I made my way to the kitchen. A third cup of coffee probably wasn't the best idea—what with my nerves so frayed—but I needed to focus. All I knew at this point regarding the show was that production would wrap up in L.A., then come Monday, they'd be headed to Squirrel Cove for the week.

That gave me close to a week to gather more information on the logging company, wildlife center, and maybe take some psychic lessons from Viv. The woman seriously needed to step up to the plate.

The startling revelation that Real Ghostly Encounters was about to descend on my little town had caused one unexpected result: I'd lost all interest in Stan's mysterious death. My inner Poirot only had enough bandwidth for Joshua at the moment.

I turned around with mug in hand, and there was Joshua standing quietly at the other end of the kitchen, leaning on the microwave with one elbow. For once, he hadn't scared the crap out of me. I counted that as progress.

I gave him a smile. "Thanks."

His brow wrinkled. "For what?"

"For not appearing out of nowhere and making my heart stop. It's appreciated."

A small smile tugged at Joshua's lips, but I could still detect a darkness in his mood. "Good, I'm glad. I was trying."

"I could tell."

After attempting to take a sip from my scorching hot coffee and almost burning my lip off, I abandoned it to the counter. I couldn't avoid the inevitable. I had to discuss the show with Joshua. It wasn't a hundred percent clear that the legendary wildlife center ghost was Joshua, but the coincidental timing was mind-boggling.

"So..." I tapped my fingers on the counter. "Why don't we head to the living room, have a chat?"

Joshua sighed. "I sense more bad news. Is it regarding the woman at the mystical shop, Viv?"

"No, nothing to do with her. But she's next on the list. We're going there today no matter what." I glanced at the clock. "We've got plenty of time, actually. She's supposed to meet up with us after the shop closes so we can have some privacy." I crossed my foot over my ankle. "Which means we can check out the wildlife center before then."

Joshua stared at his feet. "It's strange. I never realized there was such a place on the mountain. It didn't exist when I was alive."

I cleared my throat. "Uh, yeah. About that." I grabbed my mug, secure in the fact that it was likely at a drinkable temperature by now. "Let's have that talk, shall we?"

While Joshua did follow me into the next room, he did so with an air of suspicion, his gaze never leaving me as if he might miss some trick I had up my sleeve. I settled in the chair, and he took his usual spot on the sofa. I figured I'd might as well get to the heart of things and not drag out the potentially awful truth.

"So..." I took a sip of my coffee, already thwarting my own plan of not dragging my heels. "You never said anything to me in the car, and you disappeared last night, but I'm guessing you heard what Ana and I were talking about?"

Joshua's nostrils flared and he straightened, slowly crossing one leg over the other, lacing his fingers together tightly before resting them on his knee. The man was giving 'tense' a whole new meaning.

"If you're referring to the googly eyes, then yes. I heard."

I blinked several times. "You...? Oh. Well, Ana likes to joke around. You'll get used to her twisted sense of humor eventually."

I startled myself by how casually I'd let it slide out that the connection between me and Joshua would be ongoing.

"I see," he said curtly. "Then that supposedly handsome ghost investigator didn't make googly eyes at you?"

I refrained from groaning. We had much more important issues to discuss. "Do you even know what a googly eye is?"

"No. But it sounds painful. However, I didn't miss the insinuation your friend was making, what with this man being a whore and everything." Joshua turned up his nose. "I've never heard of such a thing, but I found it to be quite crass."

"Unbelievable." I bit back my anger before I continued, determined to cut him a break since this modern society stuff was still so foreign to him. "Before I respond to anything else, let's leave Ana out of this. Our girl talk was just that—for *girls*. You can have all the opinions you want, but you don't get to be snippy with me about my best friend. You don't like our conversations? Well buddy, kick rocks."

Okay, so the anger-biting was a fail. He might be having a difficult time adjusting to modern mores, but I wasn't about to let anyone diss my bestie.

Joshua's face turned scarlet, and I prepared myself for the inevitable disappearing act.

I held up my hand. "Wait. That might've come out a tad harsh, but you have to understand. I'd protect her to the death. We've always had each other's backs."

Joshua held my gaze for a few beats then slowly nodded. "I can respect that. I apologize if I offended you." He scrubbed his face with one hand. "What had me more concerned was this...this... whorish male who is clearly interested in being disrespectful toward you." He set his lips in a thin line. "Perhaps you should stay away from him."

I pinched the bridge of my nose then sucked in a deep breath. "And you're probably right about that. However, that's what I brought you in here to discuss. I'm afraid that Dirk and company will be here next week, filming the show at the wildlife center." I squirmed in the chair. "You didn't overhear that part of the conversation with Ana?"

He regarded me with a frown. "No. I left the room. I wasn't interested in hearing anything else about *Dirk*."

I sure as heck hoped that Dirk wouldn't be able to see or sense Joshua. Getting the two of them together on this side or the next seemed like a massively bad idea.

"Well, there's more to this whole show filming situation. You see..." I swallowed hard. "I've never heard about this before, but it seems there's a legendary ghost on the mountain, and *supposedly*, this ghost haunts the wildlife center."

Joshua's brow furrowed. "That's an odd place to haunt. Was this ghost killed by a local bear, perhaps?"

I'd been trying to forget about bears since Ana first implanted the thought in my brain, and I'd been so close to succeeding. I let out a sigh.

"No, that's not it. Joshua, I think they might be talking about you."

Joshua jerked back his head as if he'd been slapped. "Why would you think that?"

"Because the wildlife center is where the logging company used to be, and the ghost of the man is a lumberjack who was killed by the owner."

As I DROVE along the winding road to the wildlife center, I could tell how shaken Joshua was by my revelation. We'd barely spoken a word since then and my heart ached for him. In truth, we'd both known that the deeper we dug into his past, the more the likelihood existed that we'd uncover something upsetting.

"Joshua, I know you're upset. But we don't know anything for sure yet." I gripped the steering wheel tighter. "This supposed ghost is a local legend, but the actual existence isn't even confirmed. And just think, an actual team of investigators will be here in a few days. That could shed more light on the whole situation, right? It's a good thing."

Joshua sighed. "Is it? I can't understand why they're saying the logging company was so far from the cabin. That's not what I remember at all."

"Okay. Let's go through it again. Tell me what you remember from working the mountain, the cabin, your boss... Whatever might pertain to your death."

"This is ridiculous," Joshua growled. "The decades have eroded my memories. The pictures that exist in my mind are blurry, almost as if they happened to someone else." He clenched his fists. "I'm not sure of anything anymore."

"I'm sorry." I racked my brain trying to figure out the best way to reach him, to inspire him to at least try. "Well, we'll be seeing Viv later, maybe she can use one of her magical..." I drew my eyebrows together. "Incantations or whatever to help you remember."

He grunted. "From what you've already told me about her, it doesn't seem as though she's very helpful."

I couldn't deny the truth of his words. But after a lot of pondering, I'd decided that Viv was there for me more as a guide, that she probably didn't want to influence me on one course or the other. She wanted me to develop my *own* intuition, rather than relying on hers.

I spotted the sign that indicated the entrance to the center, then turned down the road, bumping along the uneven, crumbling asphalt toward the parking area. When I parked, I also noted the smattering of wooden picnic benches with flaking, almost non-existent paint that were likely splinter factories.

The visitor center building didn't seem to be faring much better. A fresh coat of paint and perhaps additional shingles couldn't do it any harm. I had a feeling that whatever payment they were receiving from the show had influenced their decision to allow them to film. Had they played up the old ghost stories to entice the production team to film the show there?

"Okay, let's go."

Joshua regarded me with pursed lips. "I still think this is a waste of time. If I can't remember anything about my death at the cabin, why would some location I've never heard of be helpful?"

I inhaled slowly, reminding myself that this couldn't be easy for him. "I have no idea, okay? But at least this location is related to the logging company, even if the ghost story is nonsense. There has to be more info here about your former employer than that wannabe museum in Stagecoach."

Joshua angled his body toward me, reaching out his hand then yanking it back. He'd likely remembered there wasn't a point in trying to touch me. He couldn't touch anyone.

"I apologize for my sour mood, Cate. I *do* appreciate everything you're trying to do for me. But I'll confess that your discovery about this place has me rattled."

I nodded. "Apology accepted. I was a bit rattled by this twist as well." I gave him a smile. "Come on. Let's check out this lovely tourist destination, shall we?"

Joshua smiled back. "We shall."

Since I was still an empathic novice, I wasn't entirely sure what I should be doing to tune into the location. The list of questions I had for Viv was impressive, so I hoped she'd cleared her schedule for the evening. I felt like I should be carrying a dowsing rod or a seeing stone or *something* to aid my abilities.

I had the pendant, of course. But so far, I couldn't tell if the shadow figure or the flashes of images or odd sensations were related to the necklace. I'd experienced odd phenomena regardless of whether I wore it or not.

Right before I reached the door to the center, I tripped over a piece of broken concrete that made up what was supposed to be a sidewalk. The place was lucky it hadn't been sued yet. An imaginary brochure popped up in my mind, describing the good times to be had by all. Fill your butt with splinters then break your leg while enjoying the outdoors! Don't miss out on the most dangerous location in the mountains above the Mojave Desert!

Once I stepped inside, a man older than my buddy Chester was seated behind the reception counter. No *way* was I touching this dude. I could practically see a shadow person lurking about without laying one finger on him.

"Two dollars."

Hello to you, too.

"Sure." I dug around in my purse for my wallet, then managed to retrieve two crumpled bills. "Here you go."

I waited for a receipt or little ticket but received a wave of the hand instead. "Go on."

The pinecones weren't the only things that were prickly at the wildlife center.

"Uh, I'm curious. Is there any information you can provide regarding the logging company history, or perhaps a book that details the ghost legend?"

He regarded me with rheumy eyes as if I were the most annoying person alive. "There are plaques with all the displays. Might be a booklet or something in the gift shop. Not sure."

I cast my eyes sideways to the so-called gift shop. It was comprised of a small bookshelf less than five feet from where the old guy sat. I sensed a lack of motivation in the man.

"Gotcha. Thanks."

I decided to save the exciting visit to the gift shop until later, concentrating on the displays that included rusty, antiquated logging equipment—such as two handled saws, some hooked logrollers, and axes. In addition, ephemera such as letters, pictures and even faded and fraying clothing of the time period were carefully arranged in glass cases.

Joshua gasped. "That..." He held a hand to his mouth, seemingly overcome with emotion. He pointed at one of the letters imprisoned by glass. "I wrote that. How is it possible it's preserved here?"

I glanced over my shoulder and spotted the center's greeter sitting with his eyes closed, his jaw slack. We were well across the open room, and I doubted whispering to Joshua would wake him from his snooze. I leaned in, squinting my eyes to see the paper Joshua had indicated.

My chest tightened at the opening line.

My dearest Cordelia...

"Uh-oh." My gaze traveled to the envelope displayed by its side. "It says here that it was sent in April of 1879. Was that...I mean, do you remember anything at all about what time of the year it was when you passed?"

"When I passed." He chuckled with no humor. "When I was alive, sometimes a family member would refer to someone dying by saying they had traveled to the Great Beyond. From what I can tell, I traveled all of ten feet and didn't move from there until I met you."

"Come on, Joshua. I can't imagine how upsetting this must be for you, but please try. Anything at all, no matter how minor. What can you remember from that time?" I indicated to the case. "The letter is dated the same year you died. What can you tell me about that, and is there anything else in there that might've belonged to you?"

Joshua pressed his lips together then leaned down and studied the contents. He kept his mouth fixed in a severe line and his eyebrows pinched together as his gaze moved from one item to the next. It was obvious to me how serious he was taking my request. A thread of calm filled me, a sense that we were in tune, working in harmony on the task that destiny had assigned us when we became bonded through the pendant.

"That pocket watch," Joshua pointed to the gold item with detailed etching on the front. Initials in an elegant cursive adorned the center. *JWB.* Joshua continued, "The letters stand for Joshua William Blackwood. My father gave it to me when I graduated law school. He had such high hopes for me.

Joshua shook his head. "Yes, its flooding back to me now. When it came to time for me to head out west, he begged me not to go. But it had nothing to do with losing Cordelia, or concern that I'd never find gold." Joshua turned to me, sadness filling his eyes. "He was disappointed."

I swallowed hard. "Why?"

"I was supposed to partner with him in the law firm. It was to be myself, my father and my brother, all working together to build the family name, to establish a respectable business." His eyes darkened. "Not to seek riches through manual labor with the lowlifes in the mines or panning on the rivers." Joshua sucked in a deep breath, "I brought shame upon the family."

"No, you didn't." I crossed my arms. "You were forging your own path, taking a chance instead of the easy way out. That's nothing to be ashamed of."

Joshua sighed. "Thank you, Cate. I appreciate your kindness. But in many ways, he was right. I doubt I would've died at such a young age if I'd followed the course he'd already laid out for me."

"I doubt you would've died at a young age if that ass hadn't killed you," I growled.

I was enraged on his behalf. I suppose he'd had so many years to accept the crap hand he'd been dealt, but it was still too fresh for me to set aside so easily.

Joshua continued to stare at the items in the case, things that had once been held in his physical hands. I read the letter, despite the fact that it was so personal. How many complete strangers had already peeked into Joshua's private world?

. . .

My dearest Cordelia,

As you can see, I've kept busy by building this lovely cabin on the mountain. The trees here are majestic, and the pine wood grain makes for a delightful design on the walls.

No news yet on when I can send for you. I know that must come as a disappointment, but I want to be sure that everything is to your liking upon your arrival. I desire nothing but the best for you, my sweetheart.

Please give everyone my love and know that I'll be calling for you soon.

I remain, my beloved Cordelia, your affectionate and faithful lover.

I RESISTED LETTING OUT A HARRUMPH. At least someone was faithful in their relationship, and it wasn't dear old Cordelia. Unfortunately, the letter didn't do much in the way of providing clues. The only thing it did was raise yet more questions, the biggest one being why it was in a glass case in California instead of a young woman's hands in Ohio long ago?

"Hey, wait. I just thought of something."

Joshua seemed to reluctantly drag his gaze away from the glass case before facing me. "What?"

I gestured to the case. "Cordelia never received your letter. Maybe she had no idea you still intended to bring her out here. Can you remember how long it was after you sent this letter that you discovered she was marrying your brother?"

His brow furrowed. "A lot of my memory is still hazy, but judging from the date of this letter, it was a mere few months later." He regarded me with pained eyes. "Do you suppose it was all a misunderstanding, that she assumed I abandoned her because she never received this letter?" Joshua touched his hand to his forehead. "Oh dear. Perhaps she didn't receive any of my letters."

I winced. What a terrible possibility.

"Okay, let's try to break this down. The only way you could've found out about her marriage to your brother was through a letter, right? If she never received anything from you, how would she know where to reach you?"

He ran his hand over his head. "Very true. Then she must have received at least one of my letters. I..." A frown marred his features. "Some of it is coming back to me. I began writing her once a week during the summer of 1878. That's when I first began working for Mr. Miller. I'm ashamed to admit that I was careful with my words. I never came out and said I was a lumberjack. Only that I was still on the mountain and to send letters general delivery."

"That's what you wrote about every week? That you were still working?"

Joshua frowned. "Of course not. I tried to fill the letters with subjects I thought she might find interesting. The beautiful birds, flowers, scenery, a new mercantile opening up in Stagecoach— anything to reassure her that she'd find living in the west to be pleasing."

"Makes sense. But we have to assume that at least one of those many letters made it to her. Which begs the question, why didn't this one?"

Joshua's shoulders dropped. "I simply don't know. I do have a vague memory of a young man, Tom. Tom Anderson, I believe? I'll need to think about it some more, but from what I remember, he would take everyone's letters to the post office down in Stagecoach each week, then subsequently retrieve our mail."

"Ah ha!"

I held up a finger and a loud pig snort burst from the wildlife center guy, followed by some low grumbling. It didn't sound like he appreciated being woken from his nap. I edged my way around the other side of the display so he couldn't see me.

"Don't you see?" I said. "This Tom character must've either kept or lost your letters."

Joshua shook his head. "There's no proof of that. I can barely remember him, but I can't imagine what he'd want my letters for." He sighed. "However, I'll try and recall as much as I can about him and the letters."

We continued to search the displays for more clues, but by the time we'd reached our fourth stuffed squirrel, I decided it was time to move on. All that was left were taxidermy examples of the local wildlife, including what seemed like a metric ton of birds, along with a thrilling interactive display on pine trees that didn't work. None of the buttons lit up when I matched a pinecone to a tree, so I decided all that was left was to make that highly anticipated visit to the gift shop.

Right as I rounded the corner of the last row of displays, I almost stumbled over my own feet.

Elliot Vance and Lily Gordon!

CHAPTER
THIRTEEN

I jumped back, hiding behind a room divider with flyers pinned to the cork board detailing various trail activities. Joshua hadn't noticed and was way ahead of me. Not that it mattered, since no one could see him, but he was still speaking as if I were right by his side. I couldn't very well yell out to get his attention, so I waited for him to figure out I wasn't there.

Elliot spoke curtly to the old man at the reception desk, but I could only catch bits and pieces of the conversation. The producer seemed upset that no one in charge was there yet to greet him. I surmised it was related to the upcoming shoot.

I sighed in frustration. If only Joshua would realize he was talking to air, his words wouldn't compete with my eavesdropping.

At last, Joshua seemed to notice I wasn't next to him. He abruptly halted, whipping his head around with a frown. Short of waving madly and possibly attracting the attention of the people I was hiding from, I peeked from the side of the screen, waiting for Joshua to come searching for me.

Due to the limitations of the pendant, he would realize I wasn't too far from him. His gaze landed on mine, his brow furrowing as I made a small gesture for him to come back. Joshua rushed over to me.

"Why are you lurking behind this screen? I thought you were ready to leave."

I used my index finger to make a small pointy motion toward everyone at the desk.

Joshua regarded them, then returned his attention to me. "You know those people?"

I nodded right as I was struck with the perfect idea. "Can you go listen to what they're saying then report back to me?"

Why hadn't I thought of this before? I was kicking myself for not taking him along to the studio after all. I could've had the murder versus accident question solved in an instant. Explaining how I knew what I discovered would be a challenge, but one thing at a time. I was definitely attending another shoot. My interest in Stan's maybe-murder had just spiked again.

Joshua glanced between me and them. "All right. But perhaps you can enlighten me when I return?"

"Yeah, once we're done spying, I'll tell you everything."

His eyebrows shot up. "I'm not sure I approve of this, but I'll do what you ask."

Joshua headed toward the bickering group, and I considered how I should describe to him what my scheme was. I hadn't planned on pursuing the questions surrounding Stan's death anymore. In my mind, the two mysteries weren't related, so why muddy the waters? I think part of me also worried that I wouldn't be giving proper attention to Joshua's dilemma.

I chewed my thumbnail. Although, what if this was part of the so-called fate that had drawn us together? Not only could Joshua potentially be quite helpful—the Mulder to my Scully—if he was the legendary ghost haunting the wildlife center, but that would mean the two mysteries truly were tied together.

Dirk was supposed to be psychic, right? I bit my lip. I'd felt something strange when he touched me. Maybe that was his psychic energy? Everything could be neatly tied up if Dirk and Joshua interacted at the site of Joshua's death.

I jumped behind the screen as Elliot and Lily finished with the old man then turned in my direction. *Crap.* They seemed to be headed my way, so I hurriedly tip-toed to another divider in the labyrinth of displays. I could always pretend to merely be another visitor to the center, but that wouldn't encourage them to say anything potentially incriminating in my presence.

Joshua rejoined me then pointed to another divider. "Go behind there. They're about to round this corner."

I gave him a thumbs up then did what he said. We went through this exercise a couple more times until Elliot and Lily were far from the desk. They stopped at one of the cases with a random selection of rocks and minerals that could be found on the mountain.

"This is ridiculous," growled Elliot. "This place is a joke. I don't know why I let Dirk talk me into going through with this location after everything that happened with Stan."

"Ssh! What happens if anyone finds out we were here together when Stan died?"

My ears pricked up.

An irritated sigh came from Elliot. "Don't be absurd. You stayed in our room the entire time and arrived before anyone else could see you. For the love of all that is holy, quit worrying."

"You don't think Dirk has figured out it's you I've been having an affair with this entire time, not Franco? Or Sal? Or Lucas?"

Elliot sighed again and I wondered if the man was truly that annoyed, or if he was having trouble breathing.

"I'm getting sick of all your nonsense. Stan's death will officially be declared an accident any day now. Then the way will be cleared for you to inherit his estate and we can begin being seen together. Until then, we lay low. Got it?"

"I know, baby," said Lily. "But all these rumors swirling around since Stan's death have been so upsetting. I just want this all to be over with so we can live our lives in the open."

"I promise everything will be fine, my little cuddle butt. Let's get the tour of the grounds over with. I want to make sure that Sam gets certain shots." He snorted. "It seems you get what you pay for with that director."

"Okay. I trust you, shnookums."

I hung back while they made their way out of the center. I also needed time to overcome a bout of nausea brought on by the interesting exchange of endearments.

"Well," Joshua said. "I'm not sure what that was all about. Can you please explain why we were both listening in on a very private conversation between a lady and her beau?"

"Yeah, but let's do that when we get out of here."

I peered around the divider again to make sure I wasn't seen in case I ran into Elliot at the shoot. Determining it was safe, I made my way to the front, Joshua rushing to keep up with me.

"I thought you wanted to take the trail, see if I recognized any of the terrain. Why are we leaving the center?"

I waved at the old man as I breezed out the door. We could come back another day for the two-minute gift shop perusal. Once we were outside, I verified no one else was around before answering him.

"Because Shnookums and Cuddle Butt went out the back and onto the trail."

Joshua choked out a laugh. "Ah, I see."

Once we got into the car and I was driving away from the scene of my eavesdropping crime, I finally felt as if I could exhale. Maybe I wasn't cut out for these Jessica Fletcher shenanigans. Perhaps I should limit my nosing around to Joshua's mystery.

I glanced at him sideways. On the other hand, having a partner who could brazenly march up to suspects without them knowing he was there was pretty cool. I tapped the steering wheel with my fingers. I'd already come this far with the mystery of Stan's death.

In for a penny and all that.

"Cate? Can you please tell me what's going on? Is this related to the murder you told me about?"

I was shaken out of my reverie. "Oh, right. Sorry. Real quick, though. What were they talking about when you were listening in?"

"I'm afraid I'm unfamiliar with some of what Schnoo—" Joshua cleared his throat. "I mean the gentleman squiring, err..."

"Cuddle Butt. Go on."

"From what I could tell, he was quite angry that the executive director of the center wasn't available to guide him. He referred to a location manager? I don't know what that means."

"That's the person who handles everything to do with where the show is filmed."

All my sleuthing was making me hungry. I know, I barely did anything, but still. I wasn't used to the cloak and dagger lifestyle and needed to be reinvigorated.

"I can't say that's very interesting at all," said Joshua. "What we heard after that was much more intriguing."

"Agreed."

I spotted the candy store. Some milk chocolate covered honeycomb sounded like it would hit the spot. I pulled into a space right in front of the shop, the tourist influx low during the week in the springtime. Once summer hit, it would be non-stop no matter what day of the week it was.

"I'm going to run in and grab something. I'll be right back."

Initially, I was consumed by guilt whenever I ate or drank anything around Joshua. However, he'd reassured me that it wasn't an issue because eating no longer mattered to him. Like his memories that had dimmed with time, recalling the desire for good food and drink had faded to nothing.

"*Then* you'll tell me what's going on?"

I stopped mid door handle pull and turned to him. "You seem pretty interested in this."

One corner of his mouth twitched, and he gave a one-shoul-dered shrug. "I've always enjoyed a good puzzle. That was the one thing about the law I found interesting, working out the mystery of a client's guilt or innocence. Had I found a way to combine that aspect with the outdoors, I would've had the perfect career."

"Well, what do you know?" I chuckled. "I learn something new about you every day."

Joshua made a shooing motion. "Go get your chocolate so I can hear the story about those two."

I pursed my lips at him. "And what makes you think I'm getting chocolate?"

He tilted his head as if I was joking. "When *haven't* you gotten chocolate?"

I frowned. "Never mind. I'll be right back."

Once I returned with a small white paper bag filled with sugary goodness, I decided to head up the road to a small park by the river. It tended to be less crowded during the week, so perhaps I could sit in the car and bring Joshua up to speed without passersby thinking I was talking to myself. Going home seemed pointless, since the meeting with Viv was in less than an hour. I figured I might as well stay close to town.

"Now where are we going?" Joshua sat with his arms crossed, the picture of impatience.

"Somewhere I won't be spotted carrying on a conversation with thin air."

"Understood. You could begin the story before we get there, you know."

He truly *was* interested. I should've been using him as my detective partner all along, but I figured he wouldn't care that much since Stan's death wasn't his problem. The years of Vince absentmindedly nodding while pretending to give a damn about what I was staying was still too deeply ingrained.

My cheeks heated. Not that I was comparing my relationship with Vince to Joshua. After all, it wasn't as if there were any romantic considerations.

"Sure. Those two? They knew the guy who died, the ghost investigator I was telling you about. They're also two suspects as far as the gossip mongers on the production are concerned. But no one knows they're together as a couple."

"Intriguing," said Joshua. "Clandestine lovers conspiring to kill the man who stands in the way of them receiving his fortune." He gave a quick nod. "Classic motive for murder."

I gripped the steering wheel tighter. "I bet he doesn't even love her. He's just been using her to get to Stan's money. Bastard."

"My goodness, Cate. You seem quite worked up about their affair."

"I think I have good reason." I was getting off-track. A skilled detective couldn't get emotionally wrapped up in their suspects. Didn't make for clear thinking. "But that's beside the point. More significantly, we're the only people who know about their secret relationship." I grinned. "They're definitely moving to the top of my list."

"Would you care to hear my opinion?"

Joshua's blasé tone told me already that he didn't agree with my assessment.

"Of course. A good back and forth is always helpful in solving a mystery."

"Well," Joshua began. "I don't believe they did it."

"What?" I huffed. "Why?"

"To begin with, why would Elliot have been at the mine shaft? Didn't you say it's in a mountain range across the highway? If he was planning on killing Stan, why rent a motel in Squirrel Cove then travel somewhere else?"

I scraped my teeth across my lower lip. "Because he didn't plan it. Maybe they were meeting up to decide between the two locations, and Elliot saw an opportunity and took it."

"Possibly. But if it wasn't planned, then why were they so careful not to be seen together?"

I pulled into a parking spot and killed the engine. Thankfully, other than one Jeep nearby, the rest of the trail's parking area was empty.

"Well, duh. Stan was alive and could catch them." I gasped. "You know what I need to find out?"

"You mean what *we* need to find out?" Joshua regarded me with pursed lips.

"Yes, *we*. Anyway," I continued. "If Stan and Lily had a prenup, then maybe his death was the only way she'd receive a dime. There's your motive right there."

Joshua drew his eyebrows together. "Are you referring to a prenuptial agreement?"

"Totally." The wheels were already turning in my head. "If Stan made Lily sign one before their marriage, that could be the answer."

Joshua plucked his beard. "Hmm. Very well could be. How would you find out that information?"

I let out a sigh. "I haven't a clue. Although, I bet my fellow gossipers from the crew will be present at the location shoot. Maybe one of them knows the answer to that."

Joshua nodded. "Then let's hope they do."

CHAPTER

FOURTEEN

Viv opened the door to the shop with a big grin. Her eyes weren't on me. No, the clearly ultra-psychic Viv had her gaze fixed on my ghostly roommate.

"Well, now. It sure is nice to meet *you*. Wish I could shake your hand." She elbowed me with a chuckle. "Or perhaps something else."

"Viv!" My cheeks caught fire and I ducked my head as I pushed past her into the store. "Ignore her!" I called out over my shoulder, unable to face Joshua. I had no idea what kind of mystical being she was supposed to be, other than a rather vulgar one.

I ran my hand across the top of my head, my thoughts still filled with all the possibilities of who might've killed Stan—and why. Was there someone we were overlooking? What about Lily's lovers? Was one of them in on it? Maybe Lily was playing Elliot, and not the other way around.

Even though I was primarily concerned with Joshua' mystery, the visit to the wildlife center had revived my interest in Stan's death. And now, Joshua's interest had been captured as well.

I startled as Viv snapped her fingers in front of my face. "Hello. Anyone in there?"

Right. I needed to switch gears. It was Joshua's turn, and I couldn't get distracted by other murders. As it was, I still felt badly that we hadn't spent more time at the wildlife center trying to discover additional details regarding his fate.

"Sorry." I gave her a tight smile. "I'll behave." I leaned against the counter next to the register and cleared my throat. "As you know, this is Joshua." I indicated to him. "And Joshua, this is the notorious Viv."

She arched her eyebrows, nodding her head. "Notorious, eh? I like it." She turned to Joshua. "Glad you could make it. I see you kids figured out that if she wears the pendant you can leave the cabin."

I narrowed my eyes at her. "Let me guess. You knew that all along but didn't tell me because...?"

Viv tsked. "Cate, Joshua, are either of you familiar with the concept of a spiritual journey?"

I let out an exaggerated sigh. "Is this one of those lifelong journeys or is it more akin to a weekend cruise to Baja?"

Viv squinted, tapping her chin as she gazed up at the ceiling. "I'm gonna go with somewhere in-between."

Joshua crossed his arms, a gesture I already recognized as meaning he wasn't in the mood for any nonsense. I knew how he felt.

"Miss Viv," he said. "I want to thank you for giving us your valuable time. However, I've been in limbo for well over a century. I'd like to think that I'm nearing the end of that journey and that Cate is merely here to give me that final nudge toward my ultimate destiny."

Nudge? Is that what I was to him? For whatever reason, it irritated me to think that, to Joshua, I was merely a means to an end.

155

Of course, what else would I be? We had no other connection beyond the pendant, a link that remained hazy at best.

I swallowed hard. "Yeah, poor Joshua has been trapped at my cabin for decades upon decades. No offense, but it kind of feels as though you're treating this like a game."

The air rushed from my lungs, my chest seemingly being squeezed by a giant fist. I couldn't breathe, couldn't speak, dizziness washing over me as I fought to stay conscious.

Oh my God. I'm totally having a heart attack.

"You're not having a heart attack, Cate." Viv rolled her eyes as if my fear of sudden death was all so boring. "You just got me a little teed off there for a sec." She shrugged. "But I'm over it."

"Y-you..." I pointed a shaky finger at her. "You did that?"

Joshua frowned, glancing between us both. "What's going on?" His gaze landed on Viv, and he gritted his teeth. "Don't you dare hurt her."

"Calm down, big fella. I won't do any permanent damage." Viv waved her hand around. "It's not easy being tasked with working through so many fated scenarios. Every once in a while, my ancient rage gets the best of me for a sec. But I eventually rein it back in." She chuckled. "Unless I don't feel like it, that is."

Great.

Joshua stuck his chin in the air. "I won't accept your help if it means putting Cate in danger."

Viv clucked her tongue. "I see that chivalry isn't dead after all." Viv gave me a wink. "Looks like destiny has your back, Cate."

"Yay me." All this talk of fate and ancient beings brought me back to wondering what the story was with Viv. "You must be a guardian angel, right?"

Angelic was the last description I'd associate with Viv, but I couldn't imagine what other reason she'd have for trying to help us at all.

Joshua arched his eyebrows as he regarded Viv. "You're an angel? You look nothing like the few angels I've met."

Viv laughed and I turned to Joshua, frowning. "I'm sure not all angels look alike."

Joshua shook his head. "You misunderstand. The angels I've met have a haziness to their form, as if they aren't solid, aren't in focus. Not only can I see through them, but they're in a constant state of motion, like a sail flapping in the breeze." He gestured a hand toward Viv. "That's not at all what she looks like."

"Oh." Back to square one.

Viv loudly cleared her throat. "I'm not an angel. Can we put a pin in it and move on?"

I scowled at her. "Fine. But I *will* find out what you are someday."

Joshua looked at Viv as if she'd suddenly grown a second head. "You mean she's not merely a psychic human?"

Viv smirked. "I can hear you, remember?"

Joshua coughed into his fist. "Of course. I'm still not accustomed to being able to converse with anyone, and Cate and I have been unable to speak together in public."

Viv nodded. "I get it. Learning curve." Viv arched her eyebrows at me. "Can we get on with it? Ellwyn and I are attending a rave at Stonehenge in about an hour."

I rubbed my temples. If she wasn't going to tell me what she was, I wasn't going to react to her offhand remark, let alone start wondering what Ellwyn was. So far, I'd assumed she was a local teenager who needed after schoolwork.

Wrong again.

"Sure." I drew my eyebrows together. "Now, where were we?" I snapped my fingers. "Oh right. Spiritual journey."

Viv nodded sagely. "Yes. Like the initiate seeking enlightenment, you must live your own journey, earn the right to your destiny. If I just tell you to do this or that—where is the lesson, amiright?"

Frustration built in me. "Then why are we even bothering to talk to you at all?"

Viv mock-gasped. "Rude!"

Joshua stepped between me and Viv, as if he could physically block us from each other. "Now ladies, let's try and work everything out in a calm manner."

Viv narrowed her eyes at him then turned to me. "Did he just 'now ladies' us?"

"I'm afraid so." I regarded Joshua. "Heads up. The modern woman, er...and the ancient female being, doesn't appreciate being handled like a misbehaving child."

Viv tossed an incense cone at me, and it bounced off my arm. "Watch the ancient talk. Not a fan."

I bent down to retrieve it from the floor then tossed the cone back with a frown. "Perhaps if I knew what you were..."

Joshua raised his hand like a schoolboy. "May I interject?"

"Yes, *please*," I groaned.

He regarded Viv. "I don't mean to be pushy, but I've waited so long to discover why I've been trapped on this plane. When Cate made me aware of your existence, I was hoping you could shed some insight on my situation?"

Viv spoke to me out of the side of her mouth. "He's so polite, isn't he?"

"Usually." I turned to her. "When I told you we needed your counsel, we were hoping to get some, you know, counsel?"

Viv looked at Joshua as she jerked her thumb at me. "She's much less polite."

I could see we were getting nowhere fast.

"Look," I said. "He might not mean to be pushy, but I do. Please. Pretty, pretty please with globs of sugar on top, can you give us a hint on what Joshua should do?"

Viv shook her head as if Joshua and I were as dense as rocks.

"To begin with, it's not what Joshua should do, it's what you *both* should do. He hasn't been able to do squat in a hundred and fifty years. Then you come along, put on the pendant, and poof! He's leaving the cabin, traveling to other cities, visiting me here with all those gorgeous muscles..." Viv waggled her eyebrows at him. "Did I mention a journey yet? That you needed to discover your destiny?" She tapped her chin with one finger. "Sound familiar?"

Forget incense cones. She was about to get conked on the head with one of her giant plastic dragons.

She shook her finger at me. "Violence never solves anything, Cate."

Psychic. Right.

I sighed. "Got it. Anything else you can share? It's hard to believe we've waited a week to meet with you, and these are the only pearls of wisdom you've got."

Viv jerked back her head as if affronted. "Oh, I've got plenty of pearls, little missy. Your brain would melt if I revealed all my knowledge, so you'd better check yourself."

I pressed my palms together in a praying gesture. "Please? Anything else? A half a pearl?"

She gave a jaunty wag of her head and grinned. "Sure. You caught me on a good day. I'm feeling generous."

I let out a long exhale, a glimmer of hope filling me. Viv gestured between me and Joshua.

"Because your fate is tied together, this journey belongs as much to you, Joshua, as it does to Cate. As you already know, the pendant is what brought you together, and as Cate continues to warm up her psychic engines, she'll receive more insight by wielding it."

She gave a satisfied nod. "Allow yourselves the opportunity to absorb this new reality. Be open to the signs that you are shown.

And remember..." Viv glanced between us both before continuing. "It isn't all about you. There are those who are chosen to facilitate."

I waited for her to continue, but she leaned on the counter with her elbow and folder her hands.

I gestured for her to keep going. "Facilitate what?"

Viv winked. "You'll figure it out."

Joshua and I groaned in unison.

"That it? That's all we get?"

Viv yawned. "For this round." She made a shooing motion. "Go ponder. I have a rainstorm in Poughkeepsie I must summon. Don't want to be late."

I tilted my head. "I thought you were going to Stonehenge?"

"Which is why I gotta get out of here. Way too much on my plate tonight."

Delving deeper might only send me over the edge, so I decided it was best to let it go. "But I have more questions. I keep getting these weird sensations, and I need you to tell me what they mean."

She groaned. "Engine warming up, Cate. Got it?"

I sighed. Half a pearl was right.

CHAPTER

FIFTEEN

"Yes, Hailey." I grinned, my daughter's excitement spilling over to me. "They'll be filming in Squirrel Cove all week, but Ana is here right now. I'll be going to the location with her tonight."

"Oh man," whined Hailey. "Why do I have this stupid job?"

I switched the phone from where I had it sandwiched between my ear and shoulder to the other side. "Because you want to pay your bills?"

"Mom, nobody wants to pay their bills. Maybe if I leave right after work, I can get there in time, then head back to L.A. at, like, four a.m. or something. It's only a two-and-a-half-hour drive."

My throat closed up at the thought of my daughter driving on no sleep. I managed to choke out a response. "You...you most certainly will *not*!"

She sighed. "Yeah, I guess it's a dumb idea."

Agreeing with Hailey that she was dumb was never happening, but severe admonishment over ever doing such a thing was warranted.

"Don't say you're dumb. But more importantly, *never* entertain driving on zero sleep again."

"I know, Mom. I'm just so bummed. It's totally unfair that you get to go when you don't even believe in this stuff." She huffed. "This is my jam, and not only that, but you also get to see Dirk in person. He's so yummy."

I wrinkled up my nose. I'd never thought of a man as yummy before. I suppose someone like Joshua...

I growled. Thinking of him as anything more than a soul I was somehow charged with helping was as far as my thoughts should go.

"You all right, Mom? Sounds like you have a stomachache."

Ana called out from the kitchen. "What's wrong? Are you sick?"

I rolled my eyes up to the ceiling. Keeping such a huge secret from my best friend and my daughter was exhausting.

"I'm fine, guys."

Ana peeked out from where she'd been examining the contents of my refrigerator, the door still wide open as if she were air-conditioning the cabin.

"Tell Hailey I said hi."

I gave her a nod. "Ana says hi."

"Tell her I said hi back."

I gripped the phone before it slipped off my shoulder as Joshua randomly materialized in front of me. We had an agreement about sudden appearances when I wasn't alone. While glaring at him, I answered my daughter.

"I will. But I need to run." Turning my back to the very distracting Joshua, I continued, "Can you come up this weekend?"

"Maybe. Ian and I were thinking of driving up the coast on Sunday, so it would have to be quick. Will Dirk still be there?"

"I see how it is. It's only worth the drive if there's a hot guy involved."

"*Mom.* Stop. You're making me feel guilty."

My stomach clenched. I was joking, but it clearly hadn't come off like that. I'd finally made peace with this new stage in our relationship—at least for the most part.

"I'm kidding, sweetie. I know you have a lot going on, and I'm not exactly right down the street anymore."

"As long as you know I'd totally be there if I could."

I smiled, not doubting her sincerity. "We'll see each other soon, okay? Those lemon tarts won't eat themselves."

Hailey snorted. "Damn straight."

We said our goodbyes and when I turned to face Ana, I dropped the phone. I'd completely forgotten about Joshua. Trying not to gaze in Joshua's direction, I kept my eyes fixed on Ana.

She took a slug of an energy drink then burped. "Sorry. Hey, want to grab something to eat before we hit the set? Heads up on the location shoots for this show. Not much in the way of craft service, so you can say goodbye to those mini croissant sandwiches and wraps from last week. At least we're not at a private home this time around." She grunted. "Those are even more of a pain in the butt. Even with a skeleton crew, it's difficult to maneuver around."

I tried not to consider the implications of a skeleton anything as I leaned down to retrieve my phone. When I rose, Joshua was not only still right next to her, but madly waving his hands around.

Ana furrowed her brow then looked to her left as if she could see Joshua. "What? There's not a spider or snake next to me is there?"

I smacked my forehead. "You think there's a snake dangling from the ceiling?"

"Hey. I'm not used to this wilderness lifestyle, okay?"

I crossed my arms, partly irritated with her, but more so with Joshua who was jumping around as if he had ants in his pants.

"I assure you, there aren't wilderness conditions in my kitchen. Umm..." I forced myself not to look at Joshua again. It was becoming impossible to ignore him. "So, yeah. Let's go into town and get some dinner. There are several places I think you'll like." I racked my brain for an excuse to leave. "But I need to check the shed real quick for a top I was going to wear tonight. I can't find it in my closet, so it must be with the stuff I have stored in there."

Ana grinned. "Want to look extra cute for Dirk?"

Joshua harrumphed. "Is that Mr. Googly Eyes?"

I scowled at him. "Knock it off."

Ana slammed her fists on her hips. "You don't have to be so snippy."

I shook my head, giving myself a mental slap. "Sorry, that came out wrong." I needed to get Joshua away from her immediately. "Seriously, don't know why I said that."

Ana's features softened. "I know you've been having a rough time, hon. But I'm your biggest supporter, you know that."

I smiled. "I do. You've been my rock, and I literally don't know what I would've done without you." I cleared my throat. "But, uh... I'll be right back."

I sent a pointed look Joshua's way as if willing him to follow. Although, judging from how oddly he was behaving, I didn't think he needed much encouragement.

By the time I made it to the shed and was safely ensconced in the dusty, dim six-by-six room, Joshua reappeared, his expression one of concern.

After pulling on the string to the bare lightbulb in the ceiling, I shut the door so Ana couldn't spot me from the kitchen window. I coughed into my fist, wondering if a violent allergy attack was in my near future.

"I thought we had an agreement about popping up when I'm not alone?"

"I know, and I apologize for that, but it couldn't be helped."

His features twisted into a pained expression and my gut clenched.

"What?"

He reached out like he was going to grab my shoulders then clenched his fists as he seemingly remembered he couldn't touch me. "Don't go tonight. Stay away from the set."

I drew my eyebrows together. "Why? This could be the answer to everything. Your murder—even your freedom from this purgatory you've been in. Not only that, but I could get some more clues about Stan's murderers. Now that we found out from Ana that Lily didn't have a prenup, I'm more convinced than ever she's behind his death."

I'd had a busy week. Sure, fixing the railing on my deck and painting the shed so it didn't resemble a hovel had been pushed to the side, but important progress had been made in other areas.

"None of that matters, Cate." Joshua pleaded. "It's not worth the risk."

I blinked several times. "I'm so confused. Our entire relationship is based on discovering what happened to you. Not only that, but we've been working on the mystery of Stan's death together. Why the sudden change of heart?"

Joshua pinched his lips together. "Our *entire* relationship?"

Who knew men from the 1800s could be so testy?

"Focus, Joshua. Why are you telling me this?"

He raked his fingers through his hair. "One of the angels I've spoken to in the past came to me a little while ago. They gave me a warning."

What felt like a boulder landed in my stomach. "And which angel was that? Was he carrying a scythe, possibly wearing a black hooded robe?"

Joshua visibly shuddered. "Don't say such a thing! And while I'm exceedingly concerned about your welfare, I want you to know that I don't see any shadow figures near you."

I glanced around. "That's reassuring. What about shadow figures anywhere at all?"

His brow wrinkled and he grasped his chin. "Hmm. No, I don't believe I've seen any since our visit to the museum."

I let out a loud exhale. "That's a relief." I brushed away a curl from my cheek that had escaped my ponytail. "But back to what this angel said. Because seriously, it would have to be epic for me to back out of going tonight."

"Let me begin by saying that every angel I've spoken with has been more cryptic than the last. In other words, Viv is an open book by comparison."

"Awesome."

After our less than informative visit with Viv, I sensed Joshua and I were pretty much on our own. In which case, I needed to put my psychic big girl pants on and face whatever came my way.

"Basically," began Joshua. "This angel warned me that you would meet death before the charlatan spirit hunters left the mountain."

A chill skittered up my spine. "I see." I swallowed hard. "Maybe it's a riddle of some sort? You know, he wasn't being literal?"

"Camiel made it clear you were in danger, though."

"In what way?"

"He said, 'Cate is in grave danger'."

I winced. "Did he have to use the word 'grave'?"

Joshua growled. "This is nothing to joke about. You're not going." He swiped his hands in a gesture of finality. "End of story."

My jaw dropped. "Whoa, hold on just a minute, buddy boy. You can't order me around. Haven't we been through this before? I'm an adult, capable of making adult decisions."

Most days.

Joshua pressed his lips together. "By now I would assume you realize I have your best interests at heart." He glanced to the side. "And anyway, I'm not nearly as bossy as you are."

I suppressed the urge to stamp my foot. I was still trying to demonstrate what a capable adult I was.

"Let's agree to disagree." I figured I needed to move things along. Ana was going to wonder how I managed to get lost in a space not much larger than the average closet. "Back to angelic predictions. I'm still convinced he wasn't being literal. I doubt there's anything to worry about."

I was convinced there was *plenty* to worry about, given all the weird stuff that had happened to me already, but I didn't want to miss out on going to the shoot—not when there was such a great opportunity to possibly solve two mysteries at once.

It didn't mean I wouldn't keep an eye out. I wasn't a complete idiot. But with so many people around, what possible danger could there be?

"Which brings me to another issue." I rubbed the back of my neck, banging my elbow against a box in the process. "I want you there tonight, but don't come within communicating distance."

Joshua frowned. "That's preposterous. Why bother going at all?"

"For starters, I need you to listen in on conversations like you did with Elliot and Lily. But you should also check out the area. See if it jogs any memories for you."

"Hmmph." Joshua narrowed his eyes. "Well, I agree those are all excellent reasons for me to be there. I imagine the no communication rule is because you can't control yourself when I'm around?"

I choked on my spit. "Wha—?" I shook my head with a grunt. "You are so full of yourself."

He stared down his nose at me. "I have no idea what that means."

"Yeah." I rolled my eyes. "I bet you don't." I brushed my palms on my jeans. I'd somehow managed to become coated in a thin layer of dust in the few minutes we'd been in the old shed. "Come on. Ana's going to think I was kidnapped by aliens."

"By what?"

"Nothing." I sucked in a deep breath. "Meet you at the location?"

Joshua sighed. "I take it you prefer I keep myself hidden until then?"

I smirked. "Can't control myself around you, remember?"

The corner of his mouth quirked into a smile. "Indeed."

SIXTEEN

I waved at Ronnie, the PA I'd met at the studio. It seemed to take a moment for her to make the connection from stranger to Ana's friend, but then she broke into a wide smile and waved back. After Ana's skeleton crew comment, I figured I wouldn't get to hang out with my buddies Tasha and Eric again, but I was surprised as a pink Mini Cooper pulled into the wildlife center lot, squeezing its way in amongst the haphazardly parked vehicles.

The show had taken over the wildlife center and bent it to its will.

Twilight had descended, and the crew that arrived earlier hadn't stopped running around for hours. I was doing my best to stay out of everyone's way by hanging back in the parking lot until it was time to shoot.

But one of my top suspects in Stan's murder—good ol' Elliot Vance—had arrived a few minutes earlier. I was filled with pride when Joshua trailed after him without a glance in my direction.

Okay, so maybe I was a bit bummed he hadn't looked my way at all, but at least he was following through on being my ears and eyes. Despite registering his disapproval once more over me attending the shooting, he was still on board with working out our double mysteries.

"Hey, great to see you here," Tasha said as she climbed out of her car. "Did you and Ana ride up from L.A. together?"

"Uh, no. Remember that mountain town I told you I live in?"

Tasha gasped. "What? No way! How cool is that?"

I chuckled. "Pretty cool, I guess."

Her eyes widened. "Did Dirk invite you to come to the shoot?"

Oh boy. Not this again.

"Good lord, no." I shook my head, laughing. "Ana told me the show was filming in my neck of the woods, and she came up a couple of days ago to stay at my place. I've been her chauffeur so she doesn't have to figure out where everything is." I gazed around. "And now, here we are."

"Well, I'm sure Dirk will be thrilled to see you." She winked. "He's such a horn dog."

I didn't know how to break it to her, but that wasn't an endorsement.

"I'm really only here in my official capacity as a professional lurker."

She laughed. "Well, you can be my guide right now. Do you know where Ana is set up?"

"Yeah, I'll show you." I gestured for her to follow me. "I'm surprised there isn't a hair and makeup trailer."

"On this budget?" She snorted. "Not hardly."

We made our way along the broken up concrete pathway to the trail that skirted the side of the main building. I wondered why the powers that be hadn't fixed the walkway before the crew descended upon the center. But if the rest of the organization was as lackadaisical as the guy I met at the reception desk during my visit, then I had no business being shocked.

"I kind of got that impression from Ana, too. Does that mean the show is in trouble?"

I figured as long as I had her ear, I might see what other potential clues I could uncover.

"Huh?" She was busy tiptoeing over the busted concrete sidewalk traps in her pointy-toed heels. "Oh! No, not at all. It's always been run this way. All the badly performed reenactments along with the talent insert shots are filmed at the studio. Then we low rent it on location. In the beginning, it was the producers' way of saving money."

She glanced at me sideways, her lips pursed. "Now that the show is a hit, though, all that extra cash goes to pay Dirk, Stan and the producers." She shook her head. "Not Stan anymore, of course."

"Oh? Then his wife didn't inherit his share?"

I had no idea how all this Hollywood stuff worked.

"Not his salary, no. That ended when he did. I don't know what sort of contract he had, but whatever salary he was pulling as talent would be nullified at death."

"So...is it a reasonable assumption that all the producers, as well as Dirk, would get a bigger cut with him gone?"

Tasha paused and checked our surroundings, then leaned in closer. Her obvious concern we might be overheard made me consider hiding behind a tree.

"Now that you mention it, I've been wondering the same thing. I didn't want to get Eric revved up the other day, but I overheard something at the end of the shoot last week. Sam, the director, was complaining to Elliot that he should get a raise now that Stan's cut was up for grabs. Elliot said he'd discuss it with the other producers and get back to him."

I shrugged. "That seems like a reasonable request."

"Yeah, except for the rumor that Sam is being fired after the initial series of locations are finished filming. You see, we stagger the shoots by doing four episodes back-to-back in one general area to save on expenses. I'm betting that the production team strings Sam along until those four are done. Then they hire a cheaper director."

"Wow." I could barely keep up with the ins and outs of the entertainment industry, let alone solve a probable murder. "Are you saying that any of the producers could've had the motive to off Stan? Not just Elliot?"

"That's *exactly* what I'm saying. Maybe it was all of them in on it together. Who knows?"

I tapped my chin with my forefinger. "Hmm. I suppose that's possible. Although it would be a lot of loose ends."

Tasha arched her eyebrows. "Loose ends?"

"Yeah. I mean, how many producers are we talking about?"

Tasha's shoulders dropped. "You're right. It would be three producers, Elliot as executive producer and Dirk. How could they possibly trust each other not to blab?"

"And I doubt all five of them charged Stan at once and pushed him down the mine shaft. It would make sense for only one other person to be present. That would leave a lot of room for the person, or persons, who didn't do the dirty deed to out the others in return for a reduced sentence."

Tasha gave me a wide smile. "Damn, you go girl. I didn't realize I had a real detective in my midst."

I snort-laughed. "I'm flattered, but I think my so-called detecting skills are a result of watching too many crime shows."

Tasha shook her head. "I don't know. In my opinion, a person has to have an investigative mind for that."

The sound of voices and approaching footsteps were our signal to drop the subject and keep moving. Tasha elbowed me as we started making our way along the path again.

"I don't know about you, but the longer this goes on, the more convinced I am that foul play was involved."

I nodded, glancing over my shoulder to make sure the crew behind us weren't too close.

"Agreed."

I wasn't about to confess that my ghost roomie was my investigating partner, or that I was actively searching for Stan's murderer. Playing as though I was there for the gossip and the hot host was the wiser move.

By the time we made it to the main staging area, the activity was in full swing. Ana waved at me once then went back to making sure Dirk and his cohorts were beautiful for the camera. Since they were filming in the dark most of the time, I didn't see the point.

However, once the ghost hunt got underway, there were plenty of moments when the spotlights were on as the investigators had supposedly unscripted discussions about their progress.

I rubbed my eyes with thumb and forefinger, taking special care not to smear the light touch of mascara I wore. All I could think of was that I'd better learn something earth-shattering during the course of the night. Otherwise, watching paint dry would be more interesting.

AFTER YAWNING SO WIDE I almost dislocated my jaw, I rolled my neck and checked my watch. *One a.m.* I groaned inwardly, my brain slowly suffocating from the mind-numbing boredom. How could Dirk and everyone else tolerate the endless sitting around waiting for the Ghost of the Week to appear?

I'd found an extra hard and extra freezy boulder to perch on while Dirk and his two co-investigators split up to explore different sections of the center. As time wore on, I'd begun to wonder what the deal was with the legendary haunting that was supposed to be Joshua.

I wrapped my arms around my torso, uneasiness settling in my gut. I should let it go, not stress anymore about what might happen if Dirk interacted with Joshua. That was something else I wished I'd asked her before she tossed us out of the shop.

I tensed. The cameraman and soundman who followed Dirk around when he was officially investigating, picked up a fast clip as they ran after Dirk. Something was happening and I didn't want to miss out. However, I wasn't permitted to chase after anyone in case I scared the ghosts away or broke Dirk's concentration while he was tuning in to the spirit world.

I snorted to myself. Elliot had given me all the rules and regulations before filming officially began, and it took all my resolve not to roll my eyes at him.

Craning my neck, I tried to ascertain where Dirk was. I chewed on my thumbnail out of frustration. Maybe if I tip-toed very quietly behind some trees, no one would notice? I wrinkled my nose. Yeah, I'd be more likely to break an ankle tromping around in the blackness over rocks and tree roots than discover anything interesting.

As I continued to squint and stare in Dirk's general direction, I had to wonder where Joshua was. Not knowing whether Dirk was communicating with him was about to send me over the edge.

"Cate!"

I yelped as Joshua appeared in front of me and slapped my hand over my mouth. A crewmember not too far from me gave me an angry shush.

I widened my eyes at Joshua, pointed to my mouth and shook my head. He stared at me, his brow wrinkling. We seriously needed to get some clearer hand signals together.

I then pointed at the crewmember who'd essentially told me to shut up then pointed at Joshua and made a blabbing gesture with my hand.

He smacked his forehead. "Yes, of course. Can you get closer to Dirk?"

I shook my head, making bizarre gestures with my hands that I hoped said, 'it's too dark for me to sneak over there and I'll get ejected from the shoot if I make too much noise'.

Joshua stared at me intently, his eyebrows pinched together. When I stopped waving my hands around, he shrugged.

"I have no idea what any of that meant."

I sighed and let my head fall back, then locked eyes with him. I pressed my lips together and made the blabbing motion with my hand again then pointed at him so hard, my finger pierced his ethereal body.

"*Fine.*" He shook his head. "But it would be so much better if you could witness this for yourself."

I threw my hands in the air as if to say 'duh'.

Joshua balled his fists as he glanced over his shoulder in Dirk's direction. Whatever was going on, he wasn't too happy about it.

"That snake is claiming he's communicating with me right now. Not only that, but he's telling the whole world that I stole from my boss and was shot by him as a result of my thievery." Joshua clenched his jaw. "I do not *steal*. This man is a charlatan."

The word charlatan gave me jolt. That was the word the angel used when warning Joshua I was in danger.

Joshua lowered his voice, his features softening. "I know. I didn't realize until I spoke it out loud. Cate, you must leave now. It isn't safe for you to be here."

Oh, how I wished I could have a conversation with Joshua right then.

I shook my head with intent. No way was I leaving right as something was finally happening.

Joshua covered his face with both hands then crossed his arms. "You *know* I can't intervene if someone tries to hurt you! You need to—"

His head whipped around and I jerked to attention as Dirk jogged down the path toward us, camera and sound guy on his heels. Right as he stopped not more than ten feet from us, he gave a nod to Sam.

"All right, everyone," Sam called out. "Take five while Dirk gets touched up, then we film the closing comments." He turned in my direction then pointed. "Excuse me, you are?"

"Oh, uh..." I cleared my throat. "I'm Ana Gutierrez' friend."

I'm sure he knew her last name, but I was startled by being noticed. I'd already had my wrist slapped by the shusher.

He slammed his fists on his hips. "This is a closed set. I'm going to have to ask you—"

"That's all right, Sam." Dirk smiled at me. "She can stay."

I shrank under the weight of everyone's questioning gaze. The last thing I wanted was everyone assuming I was Dirk's latest girl toy. Or worse, cougar toy.

Sam grunted. "Whatever. Let's be quick, people. I'd like to get everything wrapped up so we can get the hell out of this dirty, dreary forest."

I could tell Sam was a meticulous craftsman.

Right as a grinning Ana approached Dirk with her makeup kit, he winked at me.

Joshua growled, reminding me he was right there witnessing the entire exchange.

I turned away so no one could see me speaking. "Don't get all pissy."

"I really wish you'd quit using such odd phrases. I'm sure you must realize the connotation of that word and that a lady would never—"

I held up my hand, palm out. "Don't. I'm too tired for your antiquated commentary right now."

He frowned and I felt bad for snapping at him. "Listen, I know it's all a pile of baloney. Don't worry about that."

Joshua averted his gaze, pursing his lips. "I'm only concerned for your safety, nothing more."

"All I meant was—"

"My, my. Are you also psychic? Ana never let on."

I almost swallowed my tongue as I peered up at Dirk, the corners of his mouth tugged into a less than sincere smile.

"Who me?" I laughed shakily. "Of course not. I uh..."

I had nothing.

My face heated, likely turning beet red, but that wasn't too much of a concern in the dim surroundings. I was well back in the shadows from the outdoor spots directed at the main shooting area.

Dirk continued to regard me with a wide smile as if we were suddenly colleagues. Did that mean he truly was psychic and could sense I was, too?

"Are you getting any impressions from Joshua or Lance? Perhaps any other spirits that have yet to make an appearance?"

I waved my hands in protest. "No, really. I'm not psychic, just a *huge* fan of your work." Little did I know what an adept liar I'd become. "I was...musing out loud. That's all."

His eyebrows shot up. "I thought I heard something about all of this being baloney. My assumption was that you were picking up on an aspect of this haunting I might've missed."

Oh dear. "Like I said, I'm not in tune, as it were. You're the expert." I put on the best adoring fan expression I could manage.

Dirk laughed lightly, placing his hand to his chest. "You're too kind. But listen, if you ever feel as though you want to talk shop, I'm at your service."

"Don't you dare," Joshua gritted out.

I kept my eyes fixed on Dirk. "That's so nice of you. As I'm sure you can tell, I find this all so fascinating."

Dirk gazed at me in a manner I found unsettling. I wasn't sure whether to be creeped out or intrigued.

"Well, I'd better get back to it," he said. "We don't want Sam pitching a fit."

"We sure don't." I kept my tone lighthearted as if we hadn't just shared a bizarre exchange.

What felt like a punch to my chest hit me as Dirk squeezed my shoulder. I struggled to catch my breath as Joshua yelled my name from seemingly far away, as if he were speaking through a Victrola. Nausea threatened as a bout of dizziness overtook me.

As quickly as the sensation struck it was gone. Thankfully, it seemed like Dirk hadn't noticed my odd episode. Already he was being fussed over by Ana and Tasha, lights were being placed and boom mikes positioned. No one cared what I was doing.

"My goodness, Cate. What happened? Do you need a doctor?"

The fear in Joshua's voice was tangible, and I had to admit, I was a bit unnerved as well. I realized that whatever I'd experienced when I'd first touched Dirk had happened again.

I dipped my chin so no one could see my lips moving. "I'm fine." I whispered.

"Let's go, Cate. Please."

I felt terrible that I was upsetting Joshua so much, but I couldn't leave now. Not when there was the potential to discover so much more. I glanced up at him, his wrinkled brow and pained features driving home the guilt even more. I silently shook my head, and he lowered his gaze.

"All right, people! Everyone quiet. We're getting ready to roll."

Sam got behind the camera and someone I hadn't met stood next to it, counting down from five. When they reached two, they mouthed 'one' then pointed at Dirk.

Dirk's features morphed into a mask of great seriousness, a slight crease between his eyebrows with his mouth set in a grim line.

"Tonight, under the sliver of a moon casting a faint glow over Squirrel Cove, we've uncovered another piece of the nineteenth century puzzle that is the Mountain Wildlife Center ghost lumberjack. Who was Joshua Blackwood, really? Was he part of the notorious Smokin' Guns Smith gang that robbed stagecoaches between here and Kingman, Arizona?

Dirk swept his hand in a wide arc. "Or was he merely one of the many hapless drifters who made their way west, lured by the elusive promise of gold riches? Perhaps he was escaping a torrid past of thievery in the Midwest." Dirk folded his hands in front of him. "Given the circumstances of Joshua's untimely demise, it would seem that's the likely scenario. Until our next ghostly encounter—I bid you goodnight and happy hauntings."

"And...cut!" Sam yelled. "That's a wrap."

Dirk held up a finger. "I'd like to roll again. I think more emphasis on the darker nature of Joshua's deeds is essential. I meant to add the part with him confessing to me. That would reiterate the moment I connected with his spirit."

Joshua let out a sound like a wolf getting ready to attack. "Lying bastard!"

Sam rubbed the back of his neck, grimacing. Elliot suddenly appeared from the shadows.

"We're good." He gazed around the area, ignoring the scowl of death Dirk was sending his way. "Let's pack everything up and get out of here."

Dirk approached Elliot with a purposeful stride and for a moment, I thought he might punch him. Whatever they were discussing couldn't be heard. At least not the actual words. However, the intent was pretty clear.

Dirk was enraged.

I angled my body away from all the activity so I could speak to Joshua.

"Hey," I whispered. "Don't worry about that jerk. Like you said, he's nothing but a liar. And lots of people think this show is a joke because they don't believe in the supernatural."

"Like you?" Joshua didn't sound reassured. If anything, he came across as defeated.

"Josh..." I sighed. What could I say? I'd never been accused of a crime, had someone say such horrible things about me for—as Joshua said—the world to see. "I'm so sorry. I really am. I wish I could do something to make it better."

He quirked one side of his mouth. "Perhaps if he's found guilty of murder? That would make me rather giddy with joy."

I smirked. "I'm sure it would. However, we don't want to be falsely blaming him the way he falsely blamed you."

Joshua's brow furrowed. "You believe me, right? Because I didn't do any of the things he's accused me of. I'm not a stagecoach robber, or ne'er do well or thief. I swear."

"I believe you, Josh. *I* swear."

He favored me with a smile, and I smiled back. It seemed my reassurance had helped. It was true, though. I did believe him. Whether it was due to my psychic intuition, or good ol' common sense—everything about Joshua came off as genuine.

Right as a new bout of boredom was poised to take over, Lily came storming up the trail, making a beeline right for Elliot, who had his back to her as he spoke with Sam. I straightened, on alert for a potential firestorm.

"You don't need to say a word."

Joshua disappeared, and I knew he was headed their way. Without thinking, I rubbed my palms together. I shouldn't be so gleeful, but I sensed the upcoming show would be more exciting than the one they'd just filmed.

Right as Lily reached Elliot, Sam took a step back as if he'd been poked with a cattle prod. Elliot whirled around, freezing at the sight of Lily. His lip curled into a sneer, and he shoved the clip-board he'd been holding at a startled Sam.

I couldn't hear what Elliot had blurted out, but he grabbed her upper arm and started dragging her toward the ratty picnic bench area. I craned my neck to watch their progress, concerned for her welfare given that Elliot was still on the suspect list. Everyone around me carried on with their individual tasks, but all the side eye being employed told me they were keeping tabs on the situation as well.

Tapping my foot, I waited impatiently for Joshua to return. I also hoped Ana wouldn't finish up and want to leave before Joshua gave me all the lurid details.

Almost as soon as the thought came into my head, Ana gestured for me to 'come on' as she hoisted her work tote over her shoulder. I sucked in a deep breath, forcing myself to give in to the inevitable agony of waiting for the report from Joshua.

I joined Ana as she marched down the trail.

"Hey, slow down," I called out.

She glanced over her shoulder but didn't break her stride. "No way. I've had enough of this whole night."

I sighed in aggravation as I caught up to her. "It's dark, you might trip."

"Good," she groused. "Maybe I'll get workman's comp."

She sounded grouchier than usual. Of course, I'd never been with her on an overnight shoot before.

"What's wrong?"

"Oh, let me see. Where to begin?" Ana held up her finger. "Ah yes. Sam yelled at me for no reason every chance he got. Elliot insulted me by saying his twelve-year-old daughter is more talented than me, and finally, your boyfriend Dirk? He wouldn't stop complaining about the stupid foundation I was using that we *always* use." She huffed. "That's what's wrong."

I wanted to protest about the boyfriend remark, but I sensed she wasn't in the mood.

"You're better than all of them put together."

I wasn't just blowing smoke up her skirt. It was true.

"That's for sure." Ana snorted. "I'm second-guessing signing on for another season. I thought the drama and tension between Dirk and Stan was bad enough. But it seems even worse now that

Stan's gone." She heaved a sigh. "Oh well. A hot bath and some Z's should straighten me out."

I winced. "Shower stall only. Sorry."

Ana threw back her head. "Ugh. That's right. I'll settle for a beer then passing out." She elbowed me. "Is that doable?"

I elbowed her back. "Totally doable."

SEVENTEEN

*"*D*on't let him get away with it..."*

I jerked up with a gasp, sweat dripping down my neck as I attempted to figure out where I was. Swiping the back of my hand across my mouth, I blinked a few times, realizing I was in my bed.

The air seemed to leave the room as I replayed the voice from my dream. I frowned. Was it a dream? Trying to figure out the weird things that happened to me all the time was a challenge. I imagined I'd eventually get used to being a freak of nature, but that day had yet to arrive.

"Hey, Cate!" Ana yelled from the other side of the closed door. "You finally up? I need pancakes. Do they serve pancakes on this mountain?"

"Oh my God," I mumbled under my breath, rubbing my forehead. I'd begun to notice I'd get the beginnings of a headache whenever I experienced something out of the ordinary. That meant the voice I'd heard was probably more than a simple dream. "I'm getting up! And I'm sure we can find some pancakes nearby. They're not exactly an exotic delicacy."

"Speak for yourself."

I checked the bedside clock and groaned. It was the crack of noon, but I'd only been in bed since six that morning. The shoot hadn't wrapped up until four, and by the time Ana and I returned to the cabin, chatted and each drained a bottle of beer, a couple of hours had passed.

I also hadn't had the chance to get caught up with Joshua, and that was making me insane. He had to have something juicy to report about Lily and Elliot, and I was dying to know what it was. I stopped mid tug on my robe tie. Okay, not dying. Merely extra interested.

Ana glanced up from her phone as I entered the living room. She was relaxing on the sofa with one leg draped over the arm.

"You're not taking a shower are you?"

I jerked back my head as if I'd been slapped. "What?"

She dropped her phone on the cushion. "I'm starving. Plus, I have to be back at the wildlife center by two."

"Seriously? Don't they have to wait until dark to shoot?"

"Nope. We'll be doing some quick shots this afternoon of Dirk wandering around the trail, telling the story of Joshua's horrible fate, and pointing out significant locations they'll be investigating."

Every time someone brought up Joshua, speaking about him as if he were only important because he was a good ratings booster, it got on my nerves. Especially after all the smack talk Dirk had done.

However, the question of how old Joshua was he was when he died had been answered. Discovering that Joshua had only been thirty-four after all when his life was ripped from him was upsetting, but at least the Real Ghostly Encounters research team had uncovered that much.

"So?" Ana raised her eyebrows. "Pancakes now, shower later?"

I sighed. "Fine. Will you at least allow me to wash my pits and put on clean underwear? Maybe brush my hair?"

Ana hmphed. "You're such a diva." She made a shooing motion. "Hurry up."

After performing the most pathetic attempt at grooming in the history of the world, I drove Ana to the breakfast joint that catered to the locals. A sign hung over the register that declared 'If it's tourist season, why can't we shoot them?'. Squirrel Cove tended to prefer its own company.

I purposely left the pendant behind, which I'm sure didn't make Joshua too happy with me. He'd be as anxious to go over the shenanigans of the night before as I was, and the local café where I was breakfasting with my bestie wasn't the time. Undoubtedly, he'd be gesturing for me to hurry up and the word 'distraction' would take on new meaning.

But what I had planned for the afternoon should make up for it. Now that I knew Ana wasn't going to be glued to my side all day, I had a little excursion in mind.

Once our stack of cakes was consumed and we'd guzzled down two mugs of coffee each, I finally felt human again. A groggy human who wished they could take an all-day nap, but at least I was upright and relatively coherent.

"Ugh." Ana's hands rested on her stomach. "I take back all the bitchy stuff I said about this town. I'd move here for these pancakes alone."

"You think these are awesome, I have some lemon tarts I'd like to introduce you to."

Her eyes widened. "Shut *up*. Why are you tormenting me like this?"

I laughed then drained the last of my coffee. "Hey, I don't suppose you heard anything interesting last night during filming, did you?"

Ana broke into a wide grin. "About Dirk?"

I leaned forward, excitement thrumming under my skin. "Did

he let anything slip about Stan? Or what about Elliot? What's up with Lily showing up the way she did?"

Ana squinched up her face. "Seriously? You're still thinking about all that murder stuff?"

I cocked my head. "Of course. What did you think I meant?"

Ana batted her eyelashes, idly stirring her coffee. "Oh, I don't know. I thought you might be as interested in Dirk as he is in you."

My jaw went slack. Why was everyone trying to hook me up with this guy? Especially Ana. We'd already discussed him being a potential murder suspect, and now she was playing matchmaker?

"Hold up. You and I are talking about a guy who possibly *murdered* his friend and partner and, in your mind, that makes him prime dating material?"

Ana let out a loud sigh. "I assumed you were over that by now. Didn't you see the news? The investigation into Stan's death is complete. It was finally ruled an accident."

I held up my hands in confusion. "Where is this news you're always talking about? And more importantly, why didn't you *tell* me?"

"It's called the internet. Anyway, it was announced this morning while you were snoozing, and I was too consumed by my need for carbs to remember to tell you."

I slumped in my chair. Had I been wasting my time on Stan's death when I could've been focusing on Joshua instead? Guilt washed over me. After so many years of being stuck in limbo, some third-rate show comes along to poke into his personal life and make insulting accusations against about him, and all I can think about is being the next Sherlock Homes.

"Don't let him get away with it."

The voice from my dreams echoed so loudly in my head, I wondered if it was happening in real time.

I bit my lip. If Stan's death was accidental, what was this voice all about? I was so torn, I could barely think straight. As soon as I dropped Ana off at the set, I'd go home and discuss everything with Joshua. *Everything.* Together, we'd decide whether to drop our amateur investigating. I was ready to do whatever it took for Joshua to find peace.

"Oh, damn." Ana's voice yanked me out of my inner reverie. "We have to get a move on."

I glanced at my phone. It was a quarter to two, but the wildlife center wasn't that far down the main highway that traversed in and out of Squirrel Cove.

"We'll be fine if we leave now."

Ana rose, snatching the check off the table in an almost simultaneous move. "Rev up the engine, sister. I got this."

"I'll get the next round of pancakes."

After dropping Ana off at the center, I headed to the cabin. I hoped Joshua wasn't too cranky about me leaving him behind. When I pulled into my dirt driveway, I spotted him in the front picture window, my open curtains framing him as he glared in my direction.

So much for him not being upset.

"Hey." I attempted to sound bright and cheery as I breezed into the house, shutting the door behind me. "Great news. Ana has to be at the set all day and night. That leaves us loads of time to get caught up. Plus, I have an idea about where we can go today, unless..." I scratched behind my ear. "Well, new information about Stan has come to light, so we should discuss that, too."

Joshua stared at me with an unreadable expression, clearly displeased.

I winced. "Are you mad?"

His eyes flitted to the side. "Not mad. Merely..." He placed his hands on his hips then fixed me with a stone-cold gaze. "Infuriated."

Oops. "I'm sorry about leaving you behind this morning, and not finding a way to talk last night after we returned home. But in

187

all fairness, I did warn you that it might be difficult with Ana here, what with it being such a small space, and—"

"Cate, stop!" He scrubbed his face with one hand. "I'm not angry with *you*. I'm enraged at that disgusting show. Those things they said about me..." His features betrayed the pain he'd clearly been trying to mask. "I can't stop thinking about Dirk's awful lies or that you were there to hear them."

"Josh... I told you already, I don't believe a word he said." My heart broke for him. "The mere fact that Dirk lied about seeing you speaks volumes. What else could he do but come up with all that nonsense since he's a complete fake?" I sucked in a deep breath. "Come on, let's sit down and talk. I need to ask you something."

He followed me to our favorite spot: overstuffed chair and small sofa. I folded my hands in my lap, trying to decide how to begin. He regarded me with a quizzical expression, brow furrowed and head tilted.

"Josh?" he said, his mouth quirked in a smile. "No one ever called me by that name when I was alive, and you've been doing it a lot."

"Is that okay?" I didn't realize I'd shortened his name.

"Hmm." He poked out his bottom lip. "Yes. It seems natural when you say it."

I don't know why, but I suddenly felt awkward and self-conscious in front of him.

"Well, as long as you're sure it doesn't bother you." I plucked at invisible lint on my jeans. "Anyway, before we go into everything that happened last night, there's something we need to discuss."

"Let's do it quickly. The conversation between Elliot and Lily was quite interesting. It's been torture waiting for us to be alone so I can tell you."

I shot up my eyebrows. His giddiness threw me off. Here I was thinking he was sullen and feeling betrayed over my interest in finding out who killed Stan, and yet he sounded more excited about the latest intel than I was.

"Sure. Listen..." I licked my lips. "After the debacle of last night, I'm starting to feel as if I'm letting you down. Maybe we should let this whole Stan mystery go." I shrugged. "Besides, Ana told me at breakfast that his death has been officially ruled accidental, so what's the point? Instead of wasting time on him, we could be discovering what really happened to you. Dispel all those lies."

Joshua straightened, his eyes rounding. "But... We're so close to finding the answer, I'm sure of it. And how can we leave Stan in the same position I'm in? Especially since he has such a clearer memory of what happened to him than I have about myself."

"I know, but—" I blinked several times. "Wait. What? How would you know what Stan remembers?" I gasped. "Have you seen him?"

"Well, yes and no." Joshua wrinkled his brow. "I sensed his presence when he spoke to you this morning, and I could tell he was stuck here, like me. He was in a state of despair, wailing on about being betrayed and murdered. But so far, I've not been able to directly interact with a fellow spirit."

I threw myself against the back of the chair. "Shut the front door! That *was* him I heard in my dream." I growled. "Well, snap. Why doesn't he simply come out and say who killed him?" I straightened in my seat. "Ooh. Stan said 'him'. Don't let *him* get away with it."

Joshua held up his finger. "True. But while the person who did the deed was male, that doesn't mean there wasn't a female in cahoots."

"I take it you mean Lily?"

"Yes." Joshua's eyes gleamed. "Last night when she came storming onto the set, I followed them to that ridiculously large vehicle Elliot arrived in."

"Luxury SUV."

Joshua frowned. "Esyouvee. Is that French?"

I snort-laughed. "Uh, no. It stands for Sports Utility Vehicle. Carry on."

He pursed his lips at me then continued. "Well, he seemed intent on getting her away from everyone else. Once they were alone, she berated him over a conversation they'd had earlier. She insisted that she'd be getting Stan's money soon, and that if he didn't start treating her better, he could forget about her helping to finance the show."

"Wow."

I tried to picture the scenario. My own frustration revolved around never finding a way to get close to Elliot or Lily, never mind finding a reason to touch them. I truly believed that if that happened, I could gain some insight. If nothing else, I'd have a comparison between them and Dirk.

"That's all you have to say?" Joshua seemed disappointed, like he hadn't pleased me the way he'd thought he would.

"Just absorbing. What did you pick up from Elliot? Is he truly done with his little Cuddle Butt, or do you think that's how they normally are? You know, those types of couples who are loud and hostile all the time."

"What a dreadful existence." Joshua huffed. "I can't imagine what could be worse."

The cold, indifferent years with Vince came to mind. "I can." I let out a sigh. "Anyway, I take it that you're convinced Elliot and Lily are behind Stan's death?"

Joshua shook his head. "Not at all. In my opinion, that snake Dirk is the bastard who killed Stan, and he should pay dearly for his crime."

CHAPTER

EIGHTEEN

As we drove to the notorious mine shaft, I still couldn't believe how vehement Joshua was about Dirk's guilt. I didn't want to question his integrity, but I wondered if maybe on a sub-conscious level, he was pointing the finger at Dirk because of how much he clearly disliked the man. Not that I blamed him after Dirk's little stunt the night before.

Other aspects of the mystery plagued me as well—especially what Joshua had told me about Lily and Elliot.

"Once more," I started. "What did you hear exactly? Word for word."

Although I was thrilled to have a secret eavesdropping weapon in the form of Joshua, it sucked that he couldn't take notes or carry a recorder.

"I don't know what more I can add. It seems clear that he's only interested in being her beau for Stan's money."

I tapped my thumb against the steering wheel. The exit to the desert location with the mining shaft neared, then we'd be traveling about four miles off the Interstate. The last mile or so would be on a dirt road, according to the map. That would be all kinds of fun in the junk heap I was driving. I had a six-pack of bottled water and sunscreen in case the car crapped out on me.

The thought of joining Stan in the afterlife wasn't on my agenda.

I glanced sideways at Joshua. "I think we'll have to agree to disagree."

"What an odd statement."

I chuckled to myself, but everything Joshua told me about the night before tugged at me. His insistence that Dirk was the culprit ate at me, too. Did he have a valid reason for his conclusion? Then there were Lily's lovers. That was a possibility we hadn't even touched on yet. It all conspired to make my head spin.

As I turned off the highway, I continued to run everything through my mind. I chewed on my lip as I recalled the first encounter with Dirk, then the one the night before. Were those sensations a warning?

At the time, I assumed my reaction had to do with sensing Dirk's psychic abilities. But judging from the big, fat fake show he put on the night before, that possibility now seemed less likely.

Or...was it?

Perhaps Dirk couldn't perform on the spot when the cameras were rolling. I certainly knew all about *that*. Whenever something mystical happened to me, it would come out of nowhere with zero warning. What if Dirk was forced to embellish to keep the show interesting and the ratings alive?

I let out a groaning sigh.

"Have you reached the conclusion that I'm right?"

I shot Joshua a glare before returning my eyes to the road. "Not at all. I've come to the conclusion that this is confusing and that being a psychic is useless when it comes to solving murder mysteries."

"You shouldn't admonish yourself so harshly, Cate. Remember everything Viv told you about this being a journey.

One doesn't instantly become an expert at whatever skill they are gifted with. Even the most talented artist must study with a master."

"If Viv's my master, I'm toast."

Joshua chuckled. "She is quite the character—I'll give you that."

I almost flew past the dirt road turn-off, but caught it in the nick of time. Only a barely legible sign marked the location. We spent the next ten minutes jostling and jerking our way over the dusty, pothole-ridden road. If the car's drive shaft was still intact when we arrived, I'd be stunned.

At last, we reached our destination, judging from the myriad of *No Trespassing* signs and broken bits of yellow police tape whipping around in the desert wind. I parked off the road then climbed out of the car.

My shoulders dropped. "Damn."

Joshua appeared beside me. "I beg your pardon?"

I pointed to one of the outcroppings of rocks. "The mine has been boarded up."

The newness of the wood that sealed off the entrance indicated this was a recent development. Since I'd never been to the mine before, I had no idea if it was always closed off, or if it had been wide open.

Shading my eyes with one hand, I surveyed our surroundings. The group of rock formations were about ten feet high and approximately fifty feet across. The opening to the mine was to the far right. Other than a bunch of scrub brush and the occasional cactus, nothing else was nearby—not even a trail.

I regarded Joshua, who appeared deep in thought, his brow creased as he tugged at his beard.

At last, he spoke. "I'm not certain if I can accomplish this without you at my side, but I could try and enter the mine."

I tilted my head as I stared at the boards blocking off the

entrance. The barrier was such a close grouping of wood, it was almost as solid as a door.

"Well, I guess we won't know until you try." I turned to him. "We might as well find out for future reference, if nothing else."

He arched his eyebrows. "What was it you said to me the other night about our unusual partnership? A work in progress?"

My entire life had become the epitome of a work in progress. "Yup. That would be correct."

Joshua rubbed his palms together. "Wish me luck!"

He reappeared almost as quickly as he'd vanished.

I jumped. "Gah. What happened?"

Joshua's arms were crossed, his jaw ticking. I could tell he wasn't a happy camper.

"That was as dreadful as all the decades I spent trying to leave your cabin!"

I pressed my lips together, his raw frustration like a wave of negative emotion crashing over me. I'd begun to notice more and more that at times I could feel what he was feeling. Typically, it would happen when he experienced more extreme emotions.

"I'm sorry, Josh. I can't imagine what it's like for you." With an aggravated sigh, I considered our options. "I do have a crowbar in the car."

"As an attorney, I can't in good conscience advise that you commit a crime."

"What about in your capacity as my co-investigator?"

The corner of Joshua's mouth quirked in a smile. "Grab the crowbar."

At least security cameras were unlikely to catch me in the act out in the middle of nowhere, so there was that.

The moment I jammed the curved end of the tool between the biggest space I could find between the boards, I knew I was wasting my time. Champion bodybuilders couldn't pry those suckers open.

"Perhaps if you used leverage?"

Gritting my teeth together, I fought not to snap at him. "I *am* using leverage. As a matter of fact, I think my shoulders are in danger of popping out of their sockets."

He pursed his lips as he considered me with a wrinkled brow. "It's unfortunate I can't help you. I'm sure with the strength I possessed as a lumberjack I could have those boards pried loose in no time."

I yanked the blasted crowbar free, a small chunk of wood breaking away from the force of my tugging.

"Good for you."

After tossing the crowbar back into the trunk, I fished around for my emergency flashlight. I finally discovered it buried beneath an old bag of gym clothes that hadn't seen the light of day since dinosaurs roamed the earth.

"Are you all right, Cate?"

I rose too fast and banged my head on the open trunk hood. I turned around, rubbing my stinging skull. "Not anymore."

I'd only been a tad snippy.

Between the heat, dust, and exhaustion, I was pretty much done with this mining expedition. But we'd come this far, so I figured I should at least check out whatever interior to the mine my flashlight could reveal. However, if the batteries were dead? Then I'd be switching out the wine for tequila later on.

After playing with the switch and whacking the side of the aluminum casing, the light flickered on.

"Oh look. Something's working."

"Now, now," tsked Joshua. "We must stay positive."

I crouched a bit then placed the light to the small opening I'd made. "I am. I'm positive I'm over it."

The head of the flashlight was larger than the hole between the boards, so making room for my eyeball to share the space was a challenge. At last, I was able to close one eye and get the other one to focus on the small section of interior that was visible.

"Well?" said Joshua. "What do you see?"

"Dirt."

"That's all?"

I angled myself and the flashlight to one side, then the next.

"More dirt." I switched it off then straightened with a grumble. "This is ridiculous."

I sucked in a sharp breath, instinctively grabbing Joshua's sleeve in an effort to get his attention. My fingers collided with air, which brought me back to reality. Joshua wasn't the one who needed to hide, but I sure as hell did.

"Where are you going?"

Joshua's puzzled words met my ears as I scampered behind a group of rocks. A large dust cloud was being kicked up from down the road, which meant someone was headed our way. The age-old theory that the perpetrator always returns to the scene of the crime came to mind and I didn't want a murderer to catch me snooping around.

"What are you doing?"

"Someone's coming," I whispered.

"I'll go see who."

The words had barely left his mouth before Joshua was gone. His idea was solid, but even though I knew he couldn't interfere with anyone who might try to attack me on the physical plane, his presence was still a comfort.

Right as an alligator lizard skittered across the back of my hand and I jumped up shrieking, Joshua reappeared.

"Nothing to worry about," he reported. "Whoever it was is driving away from here. They must've come from one of those side dirt roads we saw on the way in."

I shook my hand, the sensation of Mr. Lizard's tiny claws still lingering on my skin. "You know what? Let's blow this popsicle stand. We're not getting anywhere."

"I have to disagree. I view this excursion as being quite informative."

I brushed off my jeans, but the fine sheen of dust being held in place by all my sweat would require a more vigorous approach when I got home.

"How so? I can't even tell where the shaft is that Stan fell down, or basically anything at *all*."

"We've discovered one important thing, though." Joshua gestured to the open space around us. "No one could have possibly snuck up on Stan. Those dust clouds you spotted proves that. And when we went over the reported details of the scene together, only Stan's car was found."

"Right. But the news reports also said the ground is so dry and hard, and with the wind constantly blowing the dirt around, that no discernible tire tracks could be identified. There could've been fifty cars here, and the detectives wouldn't be able to tell which one was which." I let out a defeated sigh. "Plus, we're going off what was reported in the media. I bet there's information the police held back that only the murderer would know."

"Cate," Joshua shook his head. "I'm afraid that, once again, I must disagree. The investigating parties have ruled Stan's death an accident, remember?"

"Gah." I marched toward the car then yanked the driver's side door open. "Then why are we here at all? I had four hours of sleep last night, I'm hot and irritable, a ghost was talking in my ear—"

I froze, something deep inside giving me clarity. The inner certainty I'd been waiting to appear ever since Viv insisted that I'm psychic.

"You know what?" I turned to Joshua, jabbing a finger at him. "It *wasn't* an accident. Stan came to me this morning, I'm sure of it." I exhaled, determination filling me. "Let's go. I want to get cleaned up then spend the rest of the night reviewing all the information we've gathered so far. Ana won't be back until morning, so we'll have the cabin to ourselves."

"Then what?"

I shrugged. "I might have to take things to a new level and try to meet with the detectives who worked on the case."

Joshua arched his eyebrows. "How does that work? You're not an official detective."

I smiled. "I have no idea. But that's not going to stop me from trying."

CHAPTER

NINETEEN

The final night of shooting didn't go as long, so the clock had just creeped past two a.m. as I pulled into the wildlife center's parking lot. Ana had texted that she'd be ready soon, so I figured I'd head over so we could leave the second she was done.

I turned to Joshua, who'd decided to tag along. "I'm fine, Josh. Like I said earlier, nothing happened last night. I probably said or did something that changed the outcome the angel warned you about."

He wouldn't meet my eyes. "And as *I* said, angels don't operate within the same time frames as humans. He could've meant tonight instead."

I wasn't winning this argument, but I wasn't backing down either. "Still surrounded by cast and crew. Just sayin'."

Joshua narrowed his eyes at me. "And you and I still suspect certain members of that cast and crew."

I smirked. "I thought Elliot and Lily were the picture of innocence?"

He shrugged. "Perhaps I was a tad influenced by my disdain for Dirk."

"Ya think?" *Ghosts.* Can't live with them. Definitely can't kill them. "Anyway, I'm heading up the trail now to let Ana know I'm here."

Joshua pointed to my phone resting in the console. "Can't you do that texting thing? Have her come to you instead."

I held up my hands in frustration. "How is sitting in my dark car in the forest with no one else around any safer than going to the spot crowded with people?"

"I would think it's obvious. The trail between here and there will be empty. Anything could happen."

I opened the car door. "I'm leaving now."

As I made my way up the path, I was treated to Joshua grumbling under his breath. A couple of times, crewmembers who must have finished up already passed me on the trail.

"See?" I whispered to him. "Not entirely alone."

He said nothing.

I arrived at the shooting site, the trail opening onto the clearing where the equipment and crew were located.

Ana was chatting with Tasha, both of them sitting in the camp-style folding chairs that were scattered about. She glanced up and broke into a smile, waving me over. Right as I reached them, Dirk suddenly appeared at my side. For a split second, I thought he was Joshua and almost told him to lay low until we got back to the cabin.

I can't imagine how he would've interpreted that.

"Cate, I wasn't expecting to see you back here again. Are you Ana's ride?"

"Guilty as charged."

I wondered if my remark was lost on him.

"As long as you're here, I thought I'd invite you to come along with us to a scouting excursion later today."

We'd reached Ana and Tasha, so I turned to them with a questioning gaze before regarding Dirk again. "Us?"

"I'm not going," interjected Ana.

"Me neither." Tasha stuck out her tongue. "I need off this mountain. It's covered in dirt and trees."

Ana looked at her. "Right? That's what I've been telling Cate all along."

I arched my eyebrows. "That's not what I remember. It was more along the lines of the mountain is teeming with lions and bears."

Dirk laughed lightly. "No tigers?"

What a hilarious man. Ana and Tasha stared at him with blank expressions for a beat then Ana turned to me.

"Sorry. I keep forgetting how thrilling you think this place is. But I just so happened to mention to Dirk what a history buff you are, and I guess he's going with Elliot, one of the location guys and a few other people to check out a possible spot for the next shoot." She shrugged, the picture of innocence. "Sounds like it would be right up your alley."

"Don't do it, Cate!"

I brushed the air next to me, Joshua on my opposite side from Dirk. Ana tilted her head.

"Mosquitoes?"

"Nah. Probably bats."

Ana 'eeked' and ducked. Payback was a... Well. You know.

"What do you say?" Dirk smiled at me with that 'I smell something funny' expression of his. Did women really find him that attractive? "If you're free, it should be interesting. There's a local guide scheduled to meet with us, too."

My knee jerk reaction was to tell him to beat it—in a very polite way, of course—but on the other hand, I'd be around both him and Elliot in a more casual setting. Who knew what they might let slip? I still hadn't come up with an excuse to ask the detectives about the scene of Stan's accident, or why they'd concluded it was an accident. This might be the answer to solving the mystery.

"What the heck." I smiled back. "Sounds like a plan."

"Wonderful," Dirk's grin grew wide. "We'll all be meeting at noon by that lumberjack statue in town."

"Sure," I said. "See you then."

After he made his goodbyes to us all, Ana smacked my arm. "The bat thing was a rotten trick, chica."

"That's what you get for encouraging jerk—" I coughed into my fist. "—Dirk."

Tasha barked out a laugh. "You were right the first time."

Ana huffed. "She doesn't have to marry him. What's a little harmless fun between the sheets?"

"Gross." The more I spoke to the guy, the ickier he became. "We've been through this a thousand times. Not. Interested."

"Oh? Then why did you agree to go?" She batted her lashes while Tasha laughed.

"Yes, Cate," Joshua growled in my ear. "Why did you agree to go?"

I smacked the air beside me again. "Damn mosquitoes. They just won't *stop*." I cleared my throat. "As you said, I'm a history buff. Could be cool."

Ana sighed. "True. Other than pancakes, I can't find a redeeming aspect to this freakin' town."

"Pancakes?" Tasha's eyebrows shot up. "Do tell."

While Ana fell into a rapturous description of our amazing breakfast of the day before, I pondered what my approach with Dirk and Elliot should be on our excursion. I also had to figure out how to reassure Joshua that nothing bad would happen. As I glanced in his direction, I noted his crossed arms and deep scowl.

This should be fun.

· · ·

The fight Joshua and I engaged in before I left to meet the Real Ghostly Encounters gang was brutal. We'd both steadfastly stuck to our own opinions. There was me insisting that unless the entire show had conspired to kill Stan and was now going to off me as a group, that he was being ridiculous. He came back with the same argument he'd had all along: angels don't waste their time giving fake warnings.

While I waited for everyone to show, I sat on the low rock wall that surrounded the twenty-foot-tall statue. The wood sculpture was a big tourist draw, and as I'd mused before, one that I hadn't paid much attention to over the years. Now I had to wonder. Was the town's wooden lumberjack supposed to be Joshua?

There definitely seemed to be gaps in the town's history. The period right after the logging camp shut down in the late nineteenth century up until right before World War II seemed rather vague. After I'd either solved, or had my fill of, the mystery surrounding Stan's death, I planned to delve deeper into Squirrel Cove's past.

Two trucks, including Elliot's SUV, pulled up almost simultaneously, and Dirk waved at me from the passenger side of the other vehicle, an equally enormous luxury SUV. At least I'd be traveling in style.

I waved back, glancing around as I made my way to the truck. I still wore the pendant but didn't see Joshua anywhere. I knew he was still angry with me. Particularly because he couldn't intervene on the physical plane if something terrible were to happen.

I pushed aside the unsettling thoughts the word 'terrible' invoked.

We still hadn't tested whether Joshua was compelled to be with me when I wore the pendant, or if he could choose to stay behind at the cabin. It seemed as though the cabin was home base, so to speak. I had a bad feeling that because he was so certain I was doomed and couldn't help, he'd opted to stay behind.

My stomach sank. Not because I was afraid or thought he was right. I missed him. I'd grown accustomed to him being with me on our little adventures. It felt wrong that he wasn't there.

"Hello, Cate." Dirk must've gotten rested and recharged. His smile came across more movie star bright than the wilted expression he'd displayed a few hours before. "You're a few minutes early. That's something I appreciate in a gal."

I frowned before I could stop myself. If he was trying to sound like a condescending troll, he'd achieved his objective.

Giving him a tight smile, I responded, "I didn't want to keep everyone waiting."

"Jump on in." He hooked his thumb over his shoulder. "We're waiting for Sam, then we'll be off."

I climbed into the backseat, where I was introduced to a photographer. Ken was supposed to take shots of the area so they could plan out where they'd concentrate the filming. The driver was simply 'the driver'. Apparently, Dirk didn't feel it necessary to treat the hired help as a human being.

Why had I become so hostile toward Dirk? Not that I'd felt a great affection for him previously, but now my impression of him was utter disdain.

As Dirk chattered away about our destination, I nodded in the appropriate spots while wondering if I could find an excuse to touch him. The problem was doing it in a way that wouldn't come across like flirting. That was the *last* thing I wanted him to conclude I was doing.

Once Sam arrived, he joined Elliot and the location manager in his SUV. I had to wonder how thick the ice was in *that* vehicle. But at least we were finally on our way. Worry over Joshua aside, I was looking forward to the trip. Not only from a mystery-solving aspect —I was also interested in whatever the local guide could offer about the spot.

Sure, I was sore when Ana told Dirk about my fascination with history to give him an excuse to invite me. However, I confessed to her before she went back to L.A. that I was half glad she did. A brief back and forth ensued over whether it was for Dirk or the historic value of the locale, but it was mostly done in jest.

"Driver," said Dirk tersely. "Make sure you take us all the way to the second lot that's halfway up the trail. Do you think you can figure it out? I told the guide to meet us there." Dirk glanced over his shoulder at me. "No point walking any more than we have to."

I caught the irritated expression of our poor driver in the rearview mirror. "Yes, sir."

Would it kill Dirk to be polite? I rubbed my upper arms as if I were freezing, which wasn't the case at all. Something like low-level electricity thrummed beneath my skin, affecting my nerves to the point where I felt like a hyper Chihuahua. I took slow, deep breaths to keep from squirming in my seat. I didn't want everyone to think I was doing the potty dance.

"Ah, here we are! And there's Bill Sampson now." Dirk paused mid door-open. "Or is it Will? Phil?" He shook his head. "Whatever."

I kept my eye-rolling to myself, and exited the truck, trying to shake off the weird sensation still coursing through my body. *Focus.* Solving a murder mystery and enjoying the scenic history lesson was all I needed to think about.

I stayed in the background, taking on the role of observer rather than participant. Not that anyone was interested in my opinions anyway, but that worked to my advantage. What wasn't helping, was the urge to run around in circles to work off the profusion of energy that continued to build inside me.

We reached an outlook that offered an expansive view of the desert that included the Salton Sea. I had to admit, it was quite impressive.

"And here," said our guide whose name turned out to be George. "This is where the young Victoria took her own life, jumping to her death because her father wouldn't allow her to marry a horse rustler."

A chill ran through me, and I vigorously rubbed my arms again. I spotted Dirk looking at me in my peripheral vision. I'm sure he thought I was goofy for acting as if I were freezing in the heat of the desert.

However, he was the least of my worries at the moment. The variety of disconcerting sensations I was experiencing was about to make things very awkward. I wasn't sure if I was picking up on the ghost of the poor girl who died, but it was making me nuts. If our guided tour didn't end soon, there was an excellent chance I'd be making a scene whether I wanted to or not.

Dirk moved closer to me then lowered his voice. "Are you feeling all right?"

I chuckled shakily, using every ounce of my strength to respond as if I wasn't on the verge of freaking out.

"Yeah, uh..." Clearly, I wasn't fine. Anyone with eyes could see that. "Sorry. I think my blood sugar is a bit low or something. Why don't you guys go on ahead? I'll just rest here a bit then catch up."

Everyone except Dirk regarded me with irritation.

"Good idea," said Elliot. "We don't have all day. When you think you're able, head back to the car." He checked his watch. "I want to get out of here soon."

My head became fuzzy, and I couldn't seem to put my thoughts in order. It honestly *was* like a low blood sugar attack.

Dirk crossed his arms. "If she's suffering from low blood sugar, she can't be left alone." He turned to Sam. "Do you mind waiting with Cate while I jog down to the truck? I have a granola bar and sports drink in there. I'll bring them back in a jiff."

Sam glared at Dirk and Elliot threw his hands in the air. "Perfect. Let's waste everyone's time."

I did some glaring of my own in between bouts of dizziness. How could Ana stand to work with these people?

Dirk grunted. "Must you always be such an ass, Elliot?"

"Don't start with me today," growled Elliot. "I'm not in the mood. We wouldn't be here traipsing around the desert if you hadn't insisted we scout this location. Desert shmesert. It all looks the same. What damn difference does it make where we film?"

"I beg your pardon," huffed George. "If you want authenticity, it makes a huge difference."

Elliot pressed his lips together. "Then let's get *on* with it." He turned to Dirk and snarled, "Hurry, so you can catch up after you take care of Princess over here."

If I wasn't so woozy, I would've kicked him in a very sensitive spot.

"Ignore him, Cate," said Dirk. "He's an animal."

Elliot grunted. "I'll show you animal." He made a rude gesture at Dirk while I clutched my stomach and tried not to keel over. "You don't know the *half* of what I'm capable of."

After an exchange of rather colorful language between them both, Dirk stomped away in the direction of the vehicles. The rest of the group ignored me as if I didn't exist and followed our guide to the next destination. The timing of my weird meltdown couldn't be worse. I finally had the chance to interact with two of my suspects, and I could barely string a sentence together, let alone deduce anything.

"Cate?" Someone snapped their fingers in front of my face. "Cate, should I call for an ambulance?"

That jolted me out of my daze. "Dirk?"

"Yes, 'tis I." He sat on his haunches in front of me, staring up the trail with a sneer. "I see Elliot and the rest of the merry idiots left you to your own devices."

I groaned, only then realizing that my butt and the dirt had met. I didn't remember collapsing, but hey, I was barely coherent, so how much of a shocker could it be?

"Come on, let's get you on your feet."

The moment Dirk clasped his fingers around my arm, my stomach seized, and I had to fight not to puke.

"Y-you know," I laughed shakily. "That ambulance is starting to sound like a pretty good idea."

The ship had sailed on me pretending I was fine, and in truth, I was becoming quite concerned. I'd never felt so wonky in my life.

"Sure, I'll take care of that for you." Dirk's voice had taken on a smooth edge, as if his words were made of buttercream icing. "But let's take you over here first."

"W-wha...?" He directed me closer to the edge of the outlook and my heart trip hammered. "What are you doing?"

I glanced around for my crossbody purse that I'd been wearing. My phone was inside it, however, my bag was gone.

Dirk fixed me with a steely glare, and he gave me a shake. "Tell me, Cate. When did you know I was the one who killed Stan?"

CHAPTER

TWENTY

"Let me go." I tried to yank my arm from his punishing grip, but I had no strength.

His tone had become sour rather than sweet. "You're the real deal, aren't you? Psychic? I can tell."

Dirk pulled me closer to the edge of the rocky terrain, my heels scrabbling against the loose dirt in a feeble attempt to stop him. In the meantime, Dirk kept talking as if we were merely having a polite conversation.

"Stan used to be like you. There's this way he had..." Dirk whirled his free hand around as if trying to come up with the right words. "These mannerisms whenever he was having one of his psychic revelations." Dirk squeezed my arm harder, his hateful stare boring into me. "Like you, he'd pretend. He'd keep it all for himself and act like science was behind everything. That he was some great genius, when in reality he was just a sideshow freak."

"Why do you care?" I could barely concentrate on Dirk's words, but a part of me had to know the answers I'd been yearning for before I joined Stan and Joshua on the other side. "And if you considered Stan a freak, why would you want to pretend you're psychic?"

Dirk's fingers dug harder into my flesh. "I *knew* it. You're no different than Stan was. I put on a great show for years, helped line his pockets. And how did he repay me? The day we scouted the location at the mine he said he'd had enough of my antics.

Dirk let out a derisive snort. "Antics? *I* was the draw, not him. He didn't mind collecting all those checks from the show and personal appearances for years. His sudden crisis of conscience would expose me, destroy my career." Dirk got in my face, his fetid breath fanning across my skin. "I'm sure you can understand why I couldn't allow that to happen."

"But..." I swallowed with no spit. "How could you be sure I knew."

"Like I said, I could tell from your strange behavior. Stan taught me well. Then I followed you out to the mine yesterday and snuck behind the rocks on the other road to see what you were doing. I heard you talking to an invisible presence. Is that one of your spirit guides?"

"Sort of." I licked my dry lips, my heart thudding. "I won't say anything, Dirk. I swear. No one would believe me anyway. I'm just some jealous groupie who wanted to be on the show, but you scorned me and I'm seeking revenge. We could make that story fly."

Even I didn't believe my vain attempts to plead for my life, but I had to try. I couldn't leave Hailey without her mom.

"Nothing can save you now," he spat out. "No loose ends. However, this has to look good, like you slipped." A maniacal grin spread across his face. "Like another accident."

Dirk released me then took a few steps back. I tried to make my legs move, but they were still filled with jelly. Whatever had come over me was crippling, keeping me from protecting myself.

As Dirk surged forward, the world seemed to explode around

me. I caught a glimpse of a jet-black figure rushing toward us both. Right as it reached out with a bony claw extending from the creature's black shroud, it felt as if I were hit by a train. I flew to the side, my body skidding across the unforgiving gravel before slamming into a tree near the edge of the cliff.

Air was sucked from my lungs by the impact, and I could only watch in horror as the gruesome, shrouded figure wrapped Dirk in its arms as Dirk's momentum launched him over the side. Choking and gasping, I dragged myself to the edge of the outlook. The dark figure no longer held Dirk's physical form. Instead, he cradled Dirk's struggling, shrieking spirit as Dirk's body slammed to the ground.

I screamed, covering my eyes as I turned away from the gruesome scene. Nightmares of Dirk's death would undoubtedly plague me for a long time.

Tears streamed through my fingers as I tried to make sense of what happened. I'd barely been able to control my body, to make myself move, yet I was somehow thrown clear of danger.

"Cate! Oh, dearest Cate. You're alive! Are you terribly hurt? I didn't mean to push you so forcefully."

I lowered my hands, blinking away my tears. "Joshua? I thought... That was you?"

"Yes, yes." He tried to reach for me, but to no avail. As always, what should've been contact between us was nothing but thin air. "I'm sorry I couldn't help you sooner. In those final seconds my terror built to such an extreme level I was able to gather enough energy to shove you out of Dirk's reach." He clutched his hair. "Death wouldn't allow me to intervene any sooner." Joshua gritted his teeth. "I think he was hoping for two souls today, not only one."

My body shook uncontrollably, but it wasn't from whatever had been plaguing me earlier. This felt more like shock.

"Was it Death who caused me to become so incoherent? I could barely function."

Joshua shook his head, still crouched next to me on the ground. I didn't trust myself to stand up quite yet. "No. Death can't interfere with the human world, hasten a person's demise. We'll have to insist that Viv tell us what made you incapacitated." Joshua dropped his head in his hands. "I was so terrified, Cate." He regarded me with a pained expression. "For goodness' sake, why didn't you *listen* to me?"

I sighed. "You were right, and I was wrong, okay?"

Joshua drew his eyebrows together. "I don't care about being right. The only thing that matters is that you're safe." His head jerked up. "Uh-oh. I'll see you later." He offered me a small smile. "I'll still be by your side, but I won't distract you. I'll remain invisible."

I was about to protest that I didn't want him to be invisible, that I needed to know he was there, when the sound of excited voices met my ears. I peered over my shoulder, and sure enough, there was Elliot and crew doing a comical fake run down the trail. Other than the guide, the rest of them didn't appear very hiking savvy.

Elliot skidded to a stop when he reached me. For a moment, I thought he was going to tumble over the edge and join his nemesis, Dirk.

George offered me his hand. "That lunatic tried to push you over the side! We saw everything."

"Yeah," said Sam. "The way you hurled yourself to the side before he could push you off the cliff was incredible."

Elliot craned his neck, holding onto the viewpoint sign as he peeked over the side. He wrinkled his nose. "Unbelievable." Elliot let out a long sigh. "Well, so much for *this* show. I don't think we can carry on with *two* dead hosts."

George helped me to my feet then called emergency services. I winced as I examined both of my skinned elbows. The shoulder that slammed into the tree didn't feel so great either.

Elliot put his hands on his hips as he regarded me. "Why the hell did Dirk try to kill you? Did you have incriminating photos of him or something?"

I definitely had everyone's attention. Other than the guide who was still on the phone, the rest of the group stared at me expectantly. Since I wasn't about to make any grand psychic revelations, I needed to come up with a plausible explanation.

"Uh, he somehow got it into his head that I knew he killed Stan."

The chorus of gasps included everyone but Elliot. He smirked instead, nodding.

"I had a feeling he was behind it. They've been like oil and water for years. Dirk always was jealous of Stan's abilities." He frowned. "But how did *you* know?"

"I didn't. He just thought I did."

Mostly true.

Elliot swiped the back of his hand across his sweaty forehead. "The guy's been a pain in everyone's butt for a long time." He let out another sigh. "I suppose we have to wait around until the cops show up. There goes *my* day."

What a compassionate guy.

"I can't believe this happened to you." Ana dabbed a tissue at her eyes with one hand and held my hand with the other. I was sitting up in my hospital bed in Stagecoach, still annoyed that they were insisting on keeping me overnight. "And it's all my fault. I'm the worst friend *ever*."

"Only the second worst."

Ana gasped and I grinned.

"Kidding."

She shook her fist at me. "Okay, you got me." Her shoulders dropped. "And I deserve it."

I jostled our joined hands. "Stop it. The whole time we gossiped about the murder, neither of us actually believed he did it." A white lie was worth sparing her feelings. "And like you said, the investigation was closed. How can we be expected to know more than the cops?"

The painkiller the doctor gave me was starting to take effect and I was getting sleepy. The wooziness wasn't welcome. The sensation was too close to what I'd experienced at the outlook. I still needed an explanation for that.

"Well, I'm going to make it up to you," said Ana. "I'm not leaving your side until you're better." She smirked. "It's not as if I have a job to worry about anymore."

"Sorry." I wrinkled my nose. "Have you thought about what you're going to do next?"

"Vacation in Cabo."

"Is that a profession?"

"No, but it should be."

I laughed, but my ribs were not amused. In addition to the viciously scraped elbows and sprained shoulder, I had bruised ribs. *Yippee.* Of course, a lot was to be said for escaping the literal clutches of Death.

"You look tired, hon. Do you need me to contact Hailey or your folks for you?"

"I spoke to Hailey before you got here, and my parents can wait. I can't deal with the freak out right now. All I need is Mom screaming that she's getting on a plane to come out here *immediately*." I shuddered. "That cabin isn't big enough for the both of us."

"Okay. Why don't you try and get some sleep? I'll be right here if you need anything."

What I needed was to talk to Joshua.

"Hey, do you think you can do me a huge favor?" I plastered on my biggest smile.

"Uh-oh." Ana narrowed her eyes. "But I guess I owe you. What do you need?"

"I'm starving, and the café here is closed already. They offered me one of their gross premade sandwiches, but I wasn't feelin' it."

"Gah, of course not. What do you want?"

I tried to think of what would take her the longest. "If you go one town over just off the Interstate, there's this Chinese place that's fantastic."

She arched her eyebrows. "You're messing with me, right?"

I gave her my most innocent expression. "Not at all. My treat. I promise you'll thank me later."

Ana shrugged then rose. "Okay, sister. Cough up the dough."

"Grab my card from my purse."

I pointed toward the mangled item. I didn't remember what happened, but Dirk must have ripped it from my body, because the strap was broken. After explaining to her where the restaurant was and giving her an order I didn't intend to consume, she grabbed her own bag and slung it over her shoulder.

"I'll be back in a flash." She snorted. "Hopefully."

I closed my eyes, counting to thirty before daring to contact Joshua.

"It's all right, Cate. She's gone."

All the tension in my body dissipated. "I don't know how long we have to talk, but she should be gone for at least an hour." I chuckled. "Unless we get busted by a nurse."

Joshua took the seat Ana had vacated. "How are you feeling now?"

I yawned, fighting the effects of the painkiller. *Maybe not an hour.* I figured I should quickly get to the point.

"Thank you, Josh."

He ducked his head. "Of course, Cate. You already thanked me."

215

I picked at the thin blanket. "But you were there for me, even though you were mad."

Joshua straightened. "You assumed I left you to fend for yourself with those brutes? Never! The lack of honor between those men was disturbing. All Elliot could think of was his ludicrous show that was all built on lies."

"No." I smiled. "Not all of it was lies. Stan was for real."

Joshua furrowed his brow. "And it cost him his life."

I waved my hand around. "Enough of this morbid talk." My head lolled to the side, drowsiness winning the battle in my quest to keep my eyes open. "Maybe Viv can shed some light on everything." I chuckled, not sure if I was still conscious. "For a change."

Before drifting away, I thought I heard Joshua speak softly.

"Sleep well, sweet Cate."

EPILOGUE

T*he following week...*

Viv locked the door of the shop, then pulled the shade down over the glass. Joshua and I had been waiting for the five o'clock hour so we could engage in a serious discussion with her.

I glanced at the gargoyle clock hanging on the wall behind the register next to the empty sword holder. I didn't know if she wasn't interested in selling swords anymore, or if it was on back order, but I'd yet to see one on display.

"It's only a quarter of five. Why did you lock up?"

"It's not like I'm gonna make a million bucks in the next fifteen minutes." She meandered back to the counter area where she'd pulled up a chair for me to sit in. I was still officially considered injured—at least according to Joshua. Viv hopped onto a stool next to the register. "It's safe for you to come out now, hotcakes."

Joshua appeared with a frown marring his brow. I imagined it matched mine.

He crossed his arms. "I was wondering if you could refrain from referring to me that way?"

Viv snorted. "You can wonder all you want. I won't stop you."

Joshua rubbed his eyes with thumb and forefinger. I'd been studying Viv's notes on her personally designed tarot cards for the past hour while waiting for the shop to close.

She turned to me. "Now, you're certain no one knows you're psychic? It was only that goofball who went sailing off the cliff?"

"I'm positive. But why are you worried about other people knowing if I am? I have personal reasons for keeping it a secret, but is there something else I should know?"

Viv cringed. "To be honest, you're a bit of an embarrassment."

My jaw dropped. "That's not nice!"

Joshua scowled. "It's also quite rude. Cate's been doing the best she can—especially since she's had almost no guidance."

The corner of Viv's mouth quirked. "Now who's being rude?" She patted my uninjured shoulder. "Look, kiddo. We've already been down the 'patience on your spiritual journey' road, and something isn't taking. For instance, that gamut of dizziness and fuzziness and electrical jolts and whatever the hell else you went through on that cliff?" She huffed. "That right there was uncontrolled psychic energy. You have no clue how to utilize your powers."

I shot up from my chair, gesturing to her with arms wide. "I *know*! That's what I've been trying to get through to you this whole time. Why did you keep putting me off?"

She gave a one-shouldered shrug. "It's been a while since I've counseled a fate psychic. I'm a bit rusty."

"Say what now?"

Every time I turned around these days, it was something else.

"Cate," whispered Joshua. "What's a fate psychic?"

I pinched the bridge of my nose. "I have no idea. I'm only here for the laughs."

"A fate psychic, children, is of a higher order in the metaphysical world." Viv grinned. "Not many of you guys around anymore, hence my dropping of the ball."

Finding out I was psychic was disconcerting enough, but now I was a psychic plus? Judging from how things had been going when I thought I was a regular ol' boring medium, this didn't seem like great news.

"Does this put Cate in danger?"

Joshua's tone was even, yet I could detect the fear behind his words. The more we interacted, the more in tune we became.

Viv dug around in a drawer beneath the register before retrieving a small, engraved square metal box. "No more than usual."

"Awesome." I sighed. "So, what's next? I mean, is this related to Joshua and what happened to him?"

I still secretly wondered if Viv was holding out on us, if she knew everything about Joshua's death, but wouldn't say anything for some reason.

She pointed a finger at me. "Nothing's changed there. I'm not telling you your spiritual journey is over, that now you can get all the answers to the universe handed to you on a silver platter. I'm only saying there's more weapons you need in your psychic arsenal, and it turns out I'm the one who's stuck sharing them with you."

Joshua and I exchanged glances.

"Gee, don't hurt yourself."

Viv whacked the air with one hand. "Aw, that's okay. This mountain has been boring me half to death anyway." She grunted. "Heh heh." Viv leaned forward as if she was sharing a big secret. "But you're going to have to commit a decent chunk of time each week to your studies."

"I take it you'll be my professor?"

Viv winked. "And I won't even charge you." She arched her eyebrows. "At least not money." She retrieved a light blue stone from the metal box. "You can start by sleeping with this under your pillow. It's called angelite."

I imagined I'd be beholden to her somehow, but what other choice did I have? I certainly didn't know any other fate psychic professors. But her flippant remark about death brought me back to one of the main things I'd been wondering about since my own brush with the great beyond.

"I need to know something, Viv. When Dirk tried to push me over the side of the mountain, was Death there to collect me or him?" I swallowed hard. "Or both of us?"

Viv scratched her chin. "All joking aside, Death is a tough cookie."

"I gathered that."

She frowned. "Let me finish, smarty-pants."

"Sorry. Carry on."

"As I was saying..." she looked at me pointedly. "His job isn't an easy one, and from what I hear, he's takes no joy in his task. But, you gotta work to your strengths. That said, he's not an opportunist. He was always going to take Dirk."

"Is that part of the fate aspect?"

"See, Joshua? She's catching on."

Joshua favored me with a smile. "I'd say she's doing fantastic."

Heat burned my cheeks, and as I struggled to come up with an appropriate response, someone knocked on the shop's door.

"We're *closed*!" bellowed Viv.

The knocking continued and Viv hopped off the stool with a growl. She marched to the door, turned the latch then yanked it open.

"What part of we're closed is confusing? Oh, hey Myrna. Didn't realize it was you."

Joshua chuckled. "Squirrel Cove is much more entertaining than it was when I was alive."

My throat tightened. Joshua had become such a regular and welcome part of my world, it was easy to forget that he wasn't a living man. Even if Joshua insisted he was fine whether we ever discovered how he died or not, it didn't set right with me. I'd already made a personal vow that someday—somehow—I would find the answers that would give Joshua the peace he deserved.

Viv jerked her chin in Joshua's direction, our signal that it wasn't safe to talk in front of the everyday, regular humans.

"Cate, I'd like to introduce you to Myrna Everett. She's the owner and proprietor of the Squirrel Cove Inn." Viv turned to Myrna. "And this is Cate McAllister, my protégé."

Is that what she's calling me these days? I'd discovered that with Viv, it was best to go with the flow.

"Hi," I said, extending my hand. "Nice to meet you."

The middle-aged, petite brunette smiled at me nervously. "Same. I'm sorry to bother you while you're having a meeting, but I just..." Her face crumpled. "I'm at such a loss, I don't know what to do."

"There, there," Viv patted her back. "Tell us all about it." She reached under the counter then pulled out a flask. "Peach Schnapps anyone?"

"Oh, uh..." Myrna's hands fluttered. "I really shouldn't."

Viv held the flask out to me, and I held up a hand. "I'm good. You have at it."

"Well, Myrna," said Viv, right before she took a swig from the flask. "What's cooking?"

Myrna broke into sobs then covered her face with her hands. "My Inn!"

Viv's eyebrows shot up. "I'm not sure I'm following. Are you talking about the fire in the kitchen the other day?"

Myrna jerked up her head and her jaw went slack. "How did you hear about the fire? I swore everyone to secrecy."

"Really?" Viv pursed her lips at me then returned her attention to Myrna. "Psychic, remember?"

I couldn't help the thread of jealousy that ran through me. I was nowhere near that good. But I supposed that was where the studying part came in.

"Right, of course." Myrna heaved a big sigh. "I've been under so much pressure lately. I can barely think straight." Her lip trembled. "I'm afraid...I'm afraid the poltergeist is back. I was hoping you might know of someone who could help me be rid of it."

Viv grinned then locked eyes with me. "Why, yes. I think I know just the person to help you out."

Uh-oh.

AFTERWORD

Thank you for reading *Life in the Ghost Lane*! There's plenty to come in the Spirited Midlife world, so keep an eye out for more paranormal mystery and mayhem with a touch of romance. Up next is *Great Ghosts of Fire* where Cate and Joshua are tasked to discover whether an evil poltergeist is haunting Squirrel Cove's local Inn. Can they rescue the Innkeeper from certain doom?

Printed in Great Britain
by Amazon

18946461R00132